NYANKONTON BE YOURSELF

UNINVITED COPYCAT

AMA NKRUMAH

UNA LLC

This book is a heartfelt tribute to my mother, the strongest woman I have ever known. Her unwavering love and support have shaped me in ways words cannot fully express. From my earliest days, she instilled in me the belief that I am enough, a lesson that has become the cornerstone of my life. As I reflect on her lessons and the warmth of her embrace, I realize the profound impact she has had on my journey. Each page of this book carries a piece of her spirit, a reminder of the strength and resilience she embodied. It is through her love that I find the courage to face the world, and it is my hope that this book serves not only as a beacon of light in my life but also in the lives of others who seek inspiration and strength.

CONTENTS

INTRODUCTION

In "Nyankonton Be Yourself," the hope is that every child who engages with the story will find their spirit and intellect reignited, leading them to discover their true purpose. This fictional work draws upon the everyday experiences that influence our futures, showcasing how our beliefs and morals serve as guiding lights on our journeys. It highlights the crucial role that our surroundings play in shaping who we are, as both negative and positive environments can significantly impact our growth and choices.

By reflecting on these themes, "Nyankonton Be Yourself," encourages young readers to cultivate a positive mindset and to recognize the power they hold in charting their own paths, ultimately inspiring them to embrace their potential and contribute meaningfully to the world around them.

AUTHOR'S NOTE

In the realm of fiction, this book transports readers to a vivid landscape, crafted entirely from the imagination of its author, Ama Nkrumah. Within its pages; names, characters, and events unfold are mesmerizingly distinct and unapologetically fictitious. Any semblance to actual people, places, or occurrences is purely coincidental.

Readers are encouraged to respect the author's rights and seek permission for any reproduction beyond personal use. By engaging with this literary creation, you not only embark on an imaginative journey but also contribute to the ongoing safeguarding of artistic expression.

Your understanding and respect for these rights are greatly appreciated.

CHAPTER ONE

The Matriarch

H er beauty was both enchanting and elegant, a mesmerizing combination that captivated everyone who crossed her path. With each graceful movement, she exuded an effortless charm that lit up the room, drawing the gaze of those around her and many others. None could compare to her beauty. Her beauty, unmatched and unfathomable. Her hair, a magnificent display of voluminous frizz and stubborn kinks that embodied strength and power, reminiscent of a lion in battle. Each curl and wave seemed to demand attention, swirling in a chaotic yet captivating manner. It stood tall, defying gravity and convention, much like a proud lioness ready to protect her territory. The wildness of her hair told a story of resilience showcasing a fierce personality that embraced natural beauty without hesitation.

With her brown eyes shimmering with determination, she manifested a fierce commitment empowering her children in every facet of their lives. In a realm where loyalty and courage intertwined, a fierce sense of purpose surged within her heart. She had sworn an oath to protect her King, a noble leader whose vision guided the kingdom through turbulent times. Her unwavering commitment extended not only to him but also to the future of their lineage, her precious offspring. Just as the queen protects the king in a game of chess so did she protect her own. In her eyes, the fire of protection burned bright, a beacon of hope for those she loved.

With her curvy shape she moved with eloquence and glorified in elegance. She walked majestically proclaiming I am nature and nature is me, all things; power, might, knowledge, wealth, all belong to me. Each curve conveyed a sense of allure and confidence, hinting at the power that laid within her words and expressions. When she smiled or pouted, the world seemed to pause, transfixed by the beauty and strength her lips exuded. This distinct feature not only enhanced her charm but also served as a reminder of the potent impact that simple expressions can have on the hearts and minds of those fortunate enough to behold her. Every glance at her lips told a story, revealing the depths of her character and the undeniable presence she carried with grace and poise.

The Queen was fearless, radiant, and with elegant eyes. Her blackness was not just a trait but a profound source of beauty and intelligence that defined her essence. Simply put, she encapsulated the essence of beauty, leaving an indelible impression on everyone fortunate enough to cross her path. In her, one found an inspiring blend of strength and femininity, making her the ultimate symbol of beauty and unforgettable. She was a figure of exalted power and worldwide fame who captivated the hearts and minds of her subjects. Her influence extended far beyond her kingdom, as she possessed the remarkable ability to create and nurture both her realm and its people.

Under her guidance, her lands flourished, new inventions emerged, and cultures intertwined. She inspired loyalty, and her presence was a gleam of hope for many. With each decision, she carefully weighed the needs of her kingdom, ensuring prosperity and harmony. Within the domain where the cosmos danced at her fingertips, she held the power to shape destinies and weave fates. Life itself seemed to pause, entrusting its fragile balance to her capable hands, as if she was the very embodiment of creation. She had power to create and nurture. Life rested in her hands and wielded the scepter of the universe.

The scepter she wielded glimmered with stars, each one a promise of potential waiting to be realized. With every decision she made, galaxies could thrive or perish; the weight of the universe rested on her shoulders. Yet, rather than succumb to the gravity of such power, she embraced it with grace, crafting a tapestry of existence where hope, love, and harmony reigned supreme. In her hands, the intricate threads of life intertwined, each one a testament to the magic of possibility and the relentless spirit of the universe yearning for connection. Her glory destined to outlive all glories and in her sovereignty, she created her children so valuable and powerful she gave them power and privileges to create, restore and replenish whatever came their way. Her glory stood as a beacon, destined to outlive all others and surpassed the ordinary, unfolding a narrative of strength and resilience that captured the essence of her sovereignty.

The Queen was not only a ruler but also a

Mother to her people, fostering a sense of unity and belonging. In a world formed by her love and dedication, she nurtured her children to become incredibly valuable and powerful individuals. She opened doors to endless possibilities that would empower them in their journeys. With resilience and creativity as their guiding forces, her children emerged as architects of their destinies, capable of transforming obstacles into opportunities. They carried forward her legacy, embodying the ideals of strength, creativity, and benevolence, ready to make a significant impact on the world around them. In doing so, they not only honor her vision but also empower future generations to thrive in a landscape filled with challenges and triumphs.

As Samanpa stood in the fading light of the day, her heart ached at the memory of the last and final glimpse of the Queen. The image was etched in her mind, vivid yet elusive, like a fleeting shadow that danced just out of reach. She could still see the way the sunlight had caught the glimmer in her eyes, a spark of joy that seemed to illuminate the whole world around her. Every detail - the way her laughter intertwined with the soft breeze, the gentle sway of her hair - played like a cherished melody in Samanpa's heart.

It was a moment suspended in time, filled with unspoken words and shared dreams, now forever engraved in her soul as a bittersweet reminder of what once was. In that final glimpse, Samanpa found both solace and sorrow, a profound sense of loss that lingered in the depths of her heart. As she sat in front of the eager children, her heart raced with excitement and nervousness. The day was special; she was about to share a piece of ancient truth with them through the stories that filled the pages of her book. She turned the cover, and the rich illustrations came to life, with each word, she painted a picture of connection, showing them how their lives intertwined. The children's eyes sparkled with curiosity and wonder as they absorbed not just her story, but the underlying truth that everyone is linked in this existence.

Before she uttered the first word from the book, Samanpa chanted these words:

Samanpa - Story' Story

Children - Story is a Myth and a Myth is a Story

Samanpa - Story can be true

Children - Myth can be true

Samanpa - What is story for?

Children - Story teaches us lessons from the past

Samanpa - If you don't know your past

Children - You are bound to repeat mistakes

Samanpa - What is a Myth for?

Children - Myth is a story about

nature that connects us to her.

CHAPTER TWO

God Tempers The Wind To The Shorn Lamb

The atmosphere hung thick and husky from the lingering effects of the heavy sandstorm. Dust particles danced in the air, casting an eerie glow over the terrain. Visibility was low, whilst the air felt heavy, almost suffocating, as a peculiar silence surrounded the scene, broken only by the occasional sigh of the wind. The sky loomed overhead, a persistent shade of brown thick dust suspended in the air. As she rose from the sand that had buried her, with each upward movement, she shook off the remnants of the sandstorm that swirled around her, casting a golden haze in the air and making every breath a struggle, a harsh reminder of the elements she was up against.

The scorching sunlight bore down, relentless

and unyielding, she instinctively raised her hands to shield her eyes and face from its unbearable rays, forcing her to squint in discomfort. The sun blazed overhead, its heat intensifying as she took a cautious step forward, gawking to make out her surroundings. In that moment, willpower surged through her, propelling her to push past the discomfort and adversity.

The storm was unforgiving, but so was her resolve; she was not one to back down easily. Amid the chaos, she focused on moving forward, each step a testament to her strength and resilience.

Samanpa, a young and beautiful maiden, found herself suspended in a fleeting moment, where the world around her faded into a soft blur, as her thoughts danced between dreams and the tangible present. With each heartbeat, she grappled with the striking contrast of her ethereal experience and the solid ground beneath her feet. She felt a deep yearning to capture this extraordinary moment caught between the fragility of time and the strength of her spirit, ready to embrace the journey ahead.

With each passing moment, her heart raced, filled with a sense of anticipation and hope. She kept looking expectantly towards the east. Every second stretched. At first, she felt the weight of solitude pressing down on her making her believe that she was embarking on a fruitless journey.

She searched tirelessly through the endless heap of sand, her fortitude unchanging despite the passage of time. Hours melted into days, while those days extended into weeks, and weeks transformed into months, but still, she dug deeper, her hope lingering like a mirage on the horizon. The vast expanse of sand seemed relentless, each scoop of sand was a testament to her steadfastness, a quiet promise that she would not give up until she uncovered what she had lost. The sands held secrets, and she was determined to reveal them, no matter how long it took.

After a vigorous search, she finally welcomed her faith, recognizing it as a guiding light in her life. Though circumstances had not unfolded as she had hoped, she discovered a newfound resilience within herself. With a profound sense of acceptance, she made up her mind to embrace her situation, refusing to succumb to despair. Instead, she focused on the possibilities that lay ahead, determined to find joy and fulfillment in the present moment.

The journey might be arduous, but in her heart, she knew that every step will bring her closer to a deeper understanding of herself and her faith. All by herself, yet, as the silence enveloped her, a flicker of memory sparked within her mind. She recalled the laughter they shared and the promises made under starlit skies; she was not truly alone; he was with her in spirit, guiding her through the uncertainties that lay before her. Each step taken became a testament to their shared aspirations, reminding her that even in moments of solitude, love and companionship rise above distance. Embracing this thought, she continued forward, her heart lightened, knowing that her journey was one forged together, regardless of the miles that separated them.

In a quiet corner of the world, she envisioned a small hut perched on the hill, a sanctuary where she could wait for him. With every nail she drove and each plank she secured the hut, though modest, stood as a testament to her dreams of shared laughter, whispered secrets, and a love that surpassed detachment. She began to raise flowers and vegetables. To her, nothing carries love so well as flowers, flowers will keep her love alive. Though years had passed, and seasons shifted around her, she remained steadfast in her journey. Just as nature abhors a vacuum, so too do our lives resist emptiness. Every experience, thought, and emotion contributes to the richness of our existence, proving that indeed, nothing goes into a void without leaving a mark or inviting the birth of something anew.

Samanpa stood at the crossroads of her life, the winds of fate guiding her to this precise moment. It was as if the universe had conspired to align her path on her journey. Every decision that had led her here flashed before her eyes, each moment a crucial stepping stone. Now, at this pivotal juncture, she realized that she was not just wandering through life; she was exactly where she was meant to be, poised to embrace the adventures that awaited her. With a heart full of courage and curiosity, she opened her hut on the hill to everyone who had strayed from their paths in life. By and large, she welcomed those who sought refuge, offering them a comforting space to rest and reflect. Her humble home became a sanctuary for wanderers, each arrival greeted with a genuine smile and a listening ear. She believed that everyone had a unique story, and within the walls of her hut, troubled souls could find solace and guidance.

Over time, her reputation spread, and more travelers sought her out, drawn by the promise of understanding and compassion. In this retreat from the chaos of the world, many found not just a temporary safe haven but a renewed sense of purpose. She welcomed everyone with open arms, embodying a grace that made others feel at home. Her presence seemed to draw people in, and soon her humble abode began to thrive with warmth and amity. Most of those who arrived decided to settle close to her modest dwelling, creating a close-knit community that flourished under her kind influence.

The hill, once a small hut, transformed into a vibrant community filled with the sounds of companionship and the spirit of unity. Asempakrom was more than a settlement; it was a testament to the bonds that can form when one opens their heart to others. In the heart of the small town, Samanpa transformed into a beacon of hope for the community, earning the affectionate title of "angel" among the town folks. Her compassionate nature and unshaken dedication to helping others made her a beloved figure, known for her warm smile and comforting words. Her presence not only healed bodies but also uplifted spirits, creating a profound connection.

In every life she touched, she left an indelible mark, symbolizing the true essence of both an angel and a healer. In her quest to bring comfort and joy to those in need, she often crafted soothing herbal drinks, infused with nature's bounty. Each visit to the sick became a ritual of healing, where she would share her carefully brewed concoctions, hoping to uplift their spirits and ease their ailments. The fragrant steam that rose from the cups carried with it an essence of care and compassion, creating a moment of solace amidst their struggles. As she watched them take a sip, a warm smile would often spread across their faces. For her, these gestures were not just about the herbal remedies; they were an evidence to the strength of human connection and the power of compassion, reminding all that even in the darkest times, a little bit of care could go a long way.

Asempakrom blossomed into a vibrant community, transforming from a quaint little town into a bustling area filled with life. Despite its expansion, Asempakrom retained a certain charm; a friendly atmosphere and a close-knit community. As the sun sets, the town glowed warmly, an indication to its journey from simplicity to a thriving hub.

Samanpa grew into a tall, dark, and skinny old lady, embodying a unique presence that was hard to ignore. Her stature drew attention wherever she went, and her keen eyes sparkled with wisdom gained over the years. Despite her age, she carried herself with an elegance that belied her frail appearance. She often wore flowing garments that accentuated her height, and her hair, once a deep shade, had turned silver, framing her face with an air of grace and dignity. The lines on her face told stories of laughter, hardships, and experiences that shaped her into the person she was. Children often gathered around her, enchanted by her tales of yesteryears, while adults admired her resilience and strength. In a world that often overlooked the elderly, she stood as a remarkable reminder of beauty that surpasses age.

Every morning in Asempakrom, a lively scene unfolded as the local children made their way to gather firewood for their families. Their footsteps echoed down the dirt path, filled with the laughter and chatter that brought life to the village. As children passed by her house, they waved and greeted her warmly, her heart swelling with pride at their industriousness. Each child carried a small bundle of sticks or branches, a task they had likely undertaken for years. The ritual not only served to provide warmth and sustenance for their homes but also fostered a strong sense of community and cooperation among the young ones.

The sun rose higher, casting a golden hue over the environment, as these children continued their daily mission, embodying the spirit of resilience and tradition cherished by all in Asempakrom.

The children often spoke in hushed whispers about the enigmatic woman who lived alone on the hill. Her tiny house, skillfully crafted from clay molds, stood as a unique landmark about a mile away from the bustling streets of the town. They imagined what life was like for her, isolated from the playful laughter and chatter of other families. The hill seemed to cradle her home, giving it a mysterious charm. Some said she had magical powers, while others believed she was a kind soul who simply preferred solitude. Regardless of the stories that swirled around, all the children felt a strange mix of fascination and unease about the woman and her clay abode, sometimes daring each other to venture closer, but never quite mustering the courage to knock on her door and discover the truth for themselves.

Every night, Samanpa transformed her tiny house into a warm and inviting haven as she organized a bonfire in her cozy backyard. The sparkling flames danced against the night sky, casting a gentle glow. The aroma of burning wood mingled with the sweet scents of treats, creating an atmosphere of warmth and comfort. As the stars twinkled overhead, the bonfire became a magical place making each night special in her little corner of the world.

Although she had no children of her own, her heart overflowed with warmth and kindness for the neighborhood children. Each day, as the laughter and chatter of the youngsters reverberated through the air, Samanpa would eagerly step outside her door to greet them. With a gentle smile, she would inquire about their well-being, asking about their adventures.

One day, as the children of Asempakrom were returning from their daily firewood errands, a curious sound pierced the air. Samanpa, who had just finished gathering her own share of firewood, suddenly stopped in her tracks. From a distance, she could hear the unmistakable sound of a child crying. The sorrowful wails resonating with an urgency that tugged at her heart. Concern gripped her as she quickly glanced around to locate the source of the distress. Was one of the children hurt? or had something unfortunate happened during their venture into the woods?

Driven by a mix of worry and compassion, she set off in the direction of the cries, determined to uncover what had transpired and to offer help to the child in need. The sound grew louder as she approached, where the faint outline of a small figure twisted in distress became clearer, kneeling beside the child, Samanpa gently asked what was wrong, her voice soothing and warm. With patience, she listened to the child's fears and concerns, realizing that sometimes, all it takes is someone to care and lend an ear. She discovered the source of her distress: a snake bite on her ankle, the skin around it turning an alarming shade of purple. Her mind raced with memories of the venomous creatures that slithered through the underbrush. Knowing the danger of the poisonous snake, she swiftly assessed the situation, trying to keep her composure for the sake of the other children watching in fear. She needed certain leaves for the special remedy for snake bite, and time was of the essence. She expertly navigated the narrow path, ignoring the gentle rustle of the wind.

Each step was filled with anticipation as she reached for the tender leaves. As she plucked them with care, she couldn't help but feel a sense of satisfaction, knowing that these simple herbs would alleviate the child's pain. With a handful of herbs secured, Samanpa raced back, excitement bubbling within her as she reunited with her waiting friends. As she gently rubbed the leaves in her hands, a fragrant juice began to emerge, glistening like dew in the sun. With careful precision, she squeezed the vibrant liquid directly onto the child's bite, her heart racing as she watched for any sign of relief. Almost instantly, the tension in the air lifted; the child's grimace transformed into a look of comfort.

The children gathered around, their wide eyes filled with awe as they watched her work her magic. Instantly, the ailing child, once pale and frail, transformed before their very eyes into a picture of health. Whispers of disbelief and wonder filled the air as they exchanged glances, unable to comprehend the miracle unfolding before them. "How could someone possess such a remarkable ability to heal so swiftly? The children wondered."

As they stood mesmerized, the atmosphere buzzed with curiosity and enchantment, each child hoping to glimpse the secret behind her extraordinary gift. They had never seen anything like it before; it was as if nature itself had bestowed upon Samanpa a magical gift. They felt a mixture of admiration and yearning, wanting to learn more about her unique skills that seemed to defy the very laws of nature. Right then, they weren't just spectators; they were witnessing a powerful blend of compassion and wonder. Forever changed by the experience, a smile broke out across their faces as they wiggled their toes, already eager to return home. It was a simple act of nature's remedy, a testament to the healing power found in the most unexpected places. Samanpa gathered the children around her, her voice filled with excitement as she shared a profound lesson about self-awareness.

"You see, she said, if you truly know who you

are and what you are made of, you can achieve incredible things." The children listened intently, curious about this mysterious knowledge. Samanpa encouraged them to explore their own strengths, dreams, and the unique qualities that set them apart.

"Each of you has a spark within, she explained, gesturing to each child, and by understanding yourselves better, you can light up the world around you."

The children felt inspired, eager to embark on a journey of self-discovery that promised not only personal growth but also the ability to connect with others in meaningful ways. It was a moment of realization that would stay with them as they ventured into their own identities. They were incredibly grateful to her for all the kindness and support she had shown them. They left that day not only with their friend restored but also with a newfound respect for the healing properties of nature, wondering what other secrets the world around them might hold. With renewed energy, the children set off, Samanpa swelling with joy, knowing that sometimes the smallest gestures can make the biggest difference.

After a long day, the children returned home joyously, their spirits high. With eager voices and bright smiles, they recounted the remarkable events of their adventure to anyone willing to listen. They spoke of the tally skinny old woman, a mysterious figure who lived alone in her tiny house on the hill. Her unexpected actions during their quest had captivated them, adding a layer of excitement to their story.

Friends and families gathered around, hanging onto every word as they shared the joys and surprises of their journey. It was a day that would be inscribed in their memories, not just for the gathering of firewood but for the incredible encounter with the old woman who had brought an unforeseen twist to their simple adventure. The elders of the town gathered in the square, their faces alight with joy as news of Samanpa's good deed spread through the community. They exchanged smiles and nods, each expressing their gratitude in their own way. Some shared stories of how Samanpa's actions had positively impacted their lives, while others offered warm words of thanks and appreciation.

The atmosphere was filled with a sense of unity and pride, as the townsfolk celebrated not just Samanpa's accomplishments, but the kindness that binds them all together. This moment reminded everyone that acts of goodwill often inspire a ripple effect of positivity, strengthening the bonds among neighbors and fostering a spirit of gratitude that resonated throughout the town.

CHAPTER THREE

Everyday In Thy Life Is A Page In Thy History

"Who goes for a borrowing goes for a sorrowing." The moon, often referred to as the "light of the gods," has held a profound place in human culture and mythology throughout history. Its silvery glow, casting an ethereal glow over the nighttime scenery, has inspired countless poems, tales, and works of art. Every six months, the moon graced the night sky of Asempakrom, with its luminous beauty, captivating all who gazed upon it.

The winds also whispered gently, creating a soothing atmosphere that invited one to linger outdoors. It was a time to breathe in the fresh air, to feel the warmth of the night enwrapping the surroundings. Shadows danced lightly on the ground, and the tranquility was only occasionally interrupted by the subtle rustle of nature's smaller inhabitants. Although the prospect of encountering crawling creatures added a slight edge of caution, the overall atmosphere was inviting and leisurely.

The appearance of the moon was a magical time for the children of Asempakrom, filling the night sky with a silver glow that ignited their imaginations. As twilight descended, they would rush outside, their laughter echoing against the backdrop of twinkling stars. The moonlight transformed their familiar backyard into an enchanting playground, where shadows danced and mysteries awaited. With eyes wide with wonder, they would gaze up, captivated by the moon's luminous face, sharing tales of moonlit adventures and brave knights. It was a cherished ritual, a time when the ordinary turned extraordinary, as they played beneath the celestial beacon that seemed to smile down on them.

On that enchanting night, the moon hung high in the sky, casting a silvery glow that illuminated the world below. It was so radiant that it seemed as if one could easily thread a needle by its light. The moon beacon outshone the artificial lights of the Asempakrom, creating a magical atmosphere that transformed the usual into something unusual. Shadows danced playfully as the moonlight filtered through the leaves, covering the surroundings in a tranquil embrace. The air was still, and for a moment, everything felt serene and connected under the radiant gaze of the moon, which served as a reminder of nature's beauty and power amidst the glow of manmade inventions.

Ebube was a vibrant young girl who had always possessed an adventurous spirit. Earlier that day, while on a hunt for firewood, she stumbled upon a snake coiled lazily in the grass. In her curious nature, she reached out, unaware of the danger that lurked.

The snake, feeling threatened, struck swiftly, sinking its fangs into her delicate skin. Panic surged through her as she realized the severity of her situation. Her heart raced and her mind raced even faster. Friends she went with gathered, their faces etched with concern, as they quickly screamed to alert others. The bravery and purposefulness of Ebube shone through as she fought against the poison coursing through her veins, until Samanpa hurriedly came to her rescue. That evening was a perfect reminder for Ebube to set out on a heartfelt journey to visit Samanpa, deeply grateful for her kindness and the healing she had provided.

As she ventured alone into the moonlit cornfield, the gentle rustle of leaves whispered secrets in the stillness of the night. The air was cool, and although the winds were not wild, a mysterious sense of loneliness engulfed her. Shadows of towering corn stalks loomed overhead, casting long, distorted shapes that danced with every shift of light.

Each crunch of her footsteps seemed amplified in the silence, heightening her senses and imagination. She couldn't shake the feeling of being watched, as if the very earth held its breath, creating an unsettling tension in the atmosphere. The tranquility of the night was betrayed by the creeping sensation that something lurked just beyond the rows of corn, waiting, watching. It was a haunting solitude that settled in her bones, reminding her that even the calmest nights can stir unease within the heart. Ebube approached the situation with a sense of caution rather than outright fear. While others might have felt overwhelmed or anxious, she maintained a level-headed perspective, weighing the potential risks and outcomes. Her keen awareness of her surroundings allowed her to navigate challenges thoughtfully, ensuring that she made decisions rooted in careful consideration. This measured approach did not stem from a lack of bravery; instead, it highlighted her wisdom and ability to understand that sometimes, taking a step back can be just as important as charging forward.

Ebube's thoughtful demeanor set her apart, proving that caution can be a form of strength in itself. Thus, she exemplified the notion that being wary can lead to better choices and a more profound sense of security in uncertain situations. The moonlight guided her footsteps as she walked about a mile from her house, each step filled with appreciation and warmth , but her thoughts were solely focused on expressing her gratitude to Samanpa.

She walked briskly through the cornfield, the tall stalks swaying gently in the evening breeze. The land continued out flat before the eyes, revealing a vibrant expanse of golden cornfields that seemed to dance gently in the breeze. As far as the eye could see, this rustic wonder extended for at least four acres, with stalks standing tall and proud, their bright green leaves rustling softly beneath the moonglow. She admired the vibrant green leaves, their rustling sound creating a soothing melody against the backdrop of chirping crickets. With each step, she felt a sense of freedom, moving swiftly between the rows of corn, which seemed to stretch endlessly toward the horizon.

The only path leading to Samanpa's house wound its way through tall, rustling stalks, creating a serene yet slightly phantom atmosphere. As the breeze whispered through the leaves, the sound mingled with the soft crunch of footsteps on the dirt trail, shadows danced playfully, blinking with the dying light, while the sweet scent of ripening corn filled the air. This secluded pathway, though simple, offered a unique charm, making Samanpa's home feel like a hidden gem, a sanctuary embraced by nature's bounty.

Each step taken through the field felt like

a journey back in time, where the hustle of the outside world faded away, leaving only the relaxing beauty of the countryside. Arriving at Samanpa's door, Ebube felt a surge of emotion; she recalled the moments of care and support that had meant so much during her time of need. With a smile, she knocked gently, eager to share her thanks and to remind Samanpa of the significant impact her kindness had on her recovery. It was a night of connection and gratitude, a reminder of the profound bond forged through compassion and support. As if Samanpa had a sixth sense, she emerged from her house just in time to greet Ebube before she had the chance to raise her little hand to knock. With a warm smile on her face, Samanpa opened the door, her intuition guiding her perfectly. The moment was filled with anticipation, as Ebube, a bundle of energy and curiosity, stood there ready to brighten the night with her playful spirit.

The moon shone brightly, brightening the

close bond they shared. With laughter and excitement, they embraced the moment, ready to embark on their next adventure together. It was a simple yet profound connection that turned an ordinary night into something special, showcasing the magic of friendship blossoming in the most unexpected ways. Samanpa opened her arms wide as soon as she spotted her, a broad smile lighting up her face.

"I'm so glad to see you looking so well!" she exclaimed, her voice brimming with warmth. The two shared a brief but heartfelt embrace, a moment that spoke volumes about new formed friendship. The atmosphere was filled with laughter and cheer as they settled down. Samanpa cautiously examined the site of the bite, her curiosity aroused by the subtle marks left on her skin. As her fingers delicately glided over the tender area, Ebube was enveloped in a wave of warmth that brought an unexpected comfort. With each careful stroke, Samanpa instinctively knew the right rhythm to follow, as if guiding Ebube through a path of healing. The pain began to ebb, despite the discomfort that initially accompanied the bite.

Ebube closed her eyes, surrendering to the soothing sensations, and allowing a sense of tranquility wash over her. It was as if the very act of acknowledging the wound allowed her to reclaim a sense of peace, turning a moment of distress into one of reflection and healing.

As Samanpa continued to caress the site, thoughts of worries faded, replaced by a profound appreciation for this moment of self-care amidst the chaos of daily life. Ebube felt an overwhelming sense of gratitude as she reflected on her day. At just twelve years old, she carried the weight of a world that had never shown her the warmth of compassion or the comfort of kindness. Each day unfolded like the last, filled with distant voices and cold interactions that left her feeling invisible and unvalued. She watched other children laugh and receive hugs from their families, wondering what it would be like to feel such love and acceptance.

Her heart ached for a gentle smile, a kind word, or simply someone to ask her how she was doing. Yet, deep within her, a flicker of hope remained, a desire to know what it meant to be truly cared for, to belong somewhere, and to be seen for the person she longed to become, but that all changed in a single day. The warmth of Samanpa's attention and the little acts of kindness made her heart swell with joy. It was as if a light had shone upon her life, revealing the shadows of loneliness she had known for so long. For once, she felt seen and valued, as if she truly mattered to someone. Ebube couldn't help but cherish this new connection, hoping it would blossom into something more lasting. Her heart brimmed with hope, making her realize that love and care could come unexpectedly, transforming her world for the better.

Samanpa gently stroked her hands through her thick and beautiful hair, marveling at its rich texture and vibrant sheen. Each strand seemed to shimmer under the soft light, reflecting the warmth of their shared moment. As her fingers glided through the luscious locks, Ebube smiled, feeling cherished and cared for. It was a moment of connection, an unspoken bond woven through the intimacy of touch, where words were unnecessary and love was palpable. Time seemed to stand still as they enjoyed this peaceful interlude, a reminder of the beauty found in small gestures and shared tranquility.

Ebube felt a rush of joy as she encountered a person who genuinely cared for her, a rarity that made her heart swell with happiness. The surprise of such kindness lit up her face, radiating warmth and positivity, reminiscent of the glow of the moon she had just walked beneath, it was as if the universe conspired to bring this moment of connection into her life, and her bright smile irradiated the surroundings, reflecting her inner bliss. In that instant, all her worries faded away, replaced by the comforting realization that she was not alone; Someone truly understood her. The encounter was a beautiful reminder that compassion existed in the world, and sometimes, it shone even brighter than the moonlight itself, guiding one's way through the darkest nights.

As she stood there, her countenance transformed profoundly; the once forlorn look of an orphan now gave way to an expression imbued with the pride of a princess. This rebirth did not merely alter her appearance; it resonated from within, lightening up her spirit with newfound strength and self-worth. The world around her faded, and for a moment, she embodied royalty - every graceful gesture and confident stance spoke of her resilience and tenacity. Her eyes sparkled with endurance, revealing dreams that continued far beyond the confines of her situation. She was no longer defined by her circumstances;

instead, she embraced her identity with an elegance that was all her own. Instantaneously, she was a lodestar of hope, proving that true nobility arises from within, regardless of one's origins. Samanpa was overwhelmed with joy as she gazed at the radiant smile brightening Ebube's face. It was a sight that filled her heart with warmth and excitement. At that point, she instinctively reached out, taking her hand with gentle tenderness. The connection between them deepened, as if the world around them faded away, leaving just the two of them in that blissful moment. The laughter they shared echoed through the air, a beautiful melody of friendship and joy.

Immediately Ebube stepped into the modest interior of the house, she was initially taken aback by its humble appearance. From the outside, it seemed just like a small dwelling, However, as she crossed the threshold, she was greeted by a stunning transformation that defied her expectations. The interior unfolded in a breathtaking display of artistry and warmth, with vibrant colors and intricate decorations creating an inviting ambiance. Each room revealed a unique charm, filled with personal touches and carefully curated decor that told a story of love and creativity. Ebube couldn't help but marvel at how such beauty could reside within those unassuming walls, proving that true magnificence often lies beneath the surface. This enchanting juxtaposition of outside versus inside left a lasting impression on her heart and mind.

Inside Samanpa's tiny house, one would be pleasantly surprised by the immaculate cleanliness that greeted them. Contrary to its modest and somewhat humble exterior, the interior radiated a sense of calm and order. Every corner was thoughtfully organized, reflecting Samanpa's meticulous nature.

Bright moonlight streamed through the

windows, illuminating the polished surfaces and the carefully arranged decor. The space, though compact, offered a cozy warmth. It was a true testament to the idea that beauty often lies within. In this tiny haven, simplicity met elegance, creating a delightful oasis that stood in stark contrast to the world outside. Inside Samanpa's house, a treasure trove of unique ornaments lay hidden. Unlike anything Ebube had encountered in their small town, these extraordinary pieces sparkled with stories waiting to be told. From intricately carved wooden figures to shimmering glass sculptures that caught the light just right, every item seemed to hold a piece of Samanpa's soul. For Ebube, entering Samanpa's world felt like stepping into a mystical realm, where artistry and imagination merged.

Ebube stood in awe, her eyes wide with disbelief as she took in the sight before her. The vibrant colors, intricate designs, and peculiar artifacts scattered throughout the room left her utterly mesmerized. She had never encountered such an arrangement in her own home, nor had she ever seen anything quite like it at her friend's house. This space throbbed with an energy that was both foreign and exhilarating. Every corner seemed to tell a story, each object whispering secrets of distant lands and cultures she could only imagine. As she stepped further inside, Ebube felt as if she had entered a magical realm, one that ignited her curiosity and sparked her imagination. This was a place unlike any other, and she knew it would forever hold a special place in her heart, leaving her awe-inspired and longing for more glimpses into the beauty that lay within those walls.

Ebube's eyes darted across the room, captivated by every detail that surrounded her. The vibrant colors of the walls, the soft glow of the light fixtures, and the scattered objects all caught her attention, each inviting her to explore further. In a fit of childlike exuberance, she twirled her body, her laughter filling the air as she spun faster and faster. With each rotation, the world around her blurred into a whirlwind of shapes and colors, heightening her sense of excitement. However, the exhilaration soon turned into a dizzying sensation that washed over her, causing her to pause for a moment and breathe deeply. As she steadied herself, she couldn't help but smile, embracing the fleeting magic of the moment that transformed an ordinary room into a realm of wonder and joy.

As she stood in the center of the room, a sense of wonder enfolded her. The ornate furniture, delicately crafted with intricate designs, seemed to whisper tales from a bygone era. Rich tapestries adorned the walls, their colors opulent and bold, transporting her to another time entirely. Each object, from the gleaming chandeliers to the vintage curiosities lining the shelves, felt out of place in her modern world. It was as if she had crossed a threshold into a different life, one filled with elegance and charm that had long been forgotten.

The air was thick with nostalgia, and she couldn't shake the feeling that the room held secrets waiting to be uncovered. All at once, she was captivated in the magic of the exceptional surroundings, which seemed to defy the boundaries of time. As she marveled at the beautiful chest adorned with mysterious inscriptions, her heart raced with excitement. Her captivating eyes sparkled with curiosity, driving her to sprint towards the treasure that lay ahead. Each step brought her closer to unraveling the secrets hidden within its weathered surface. Just as she reached the chest, she encountered Samanpa, who seemed to materialize from thin air. Their eyes met, a blend of wonder and anticipation filling the air between them.

Together, they stood before the enchanting object, a silent agreement forming as they prepared to explore the unknown. What stories lay within? what adventures awaited them?. The thrill of discovery bonded them on that occasion, igniting a shared quest fueled by their adventurous spirits. Samanpa gently beckoned her closer. "Now, let us get to what I wanted to show you, my dear child," she said, her voice filled with excitement. The air was thick with anticipation as she revealed a small, intricately carved wooden box, its surface adorned with delicate patterns that seemed to dance in the fading light. With each passing moment, Ebube's eyes widened in wonder, eager to uncover the secrets nestled within. Samanpa smiled, knowing that this was not just an object but a treasure trove of stories and lessons, a bridge to the past that would connect them both in ways words could never fully express.

As the evening shadows lengthened, the bond between them grew stronger, illuminated by the shared adventure that awaited inside the mysterious box. Samanpa's fingers brushed against the ornate chest, the hinges creaking softly as she lifted the lid. Inside, the glimmer of a necklace caught her eye, its intricate design mesmerizing. As she delicately handled it, she felt the weight of Ebube's gaze upon her, a perceptible longing intertwined with curiosity.

The necklace seemed to hold secrets of its own, drawing both Samanpa and Ebube closer to its allure. It was more than just an ornament; it represented a connection, a story waiting to be unveiled. Ebube could hardly look away, the spark of fascination igniting a desire to understand the significance behind this beautiful piece. Moments ticked by as Samanpa slowly revealed the necklace, a symbolic gesture that held the unspoken words between them, bridging the gap of their thoughts in that quiet, and enchanting moment.

As she beckoned her closer, a sense of anticipation filled the air. "This is what I had in mind to show you," she whispered, a hint of excitement in her voice. "Come closer and see what is inside for yourself," she encouraged, inviting her to peer deeper into the mystery. As she leaned in, the vibrant colors and intricate details began to reveal themselves, sparking curiosity and wonder. It was more than just an object; it was a glimpse into a world waiting to be discovered, a treasure trove of stories and secrets just waiting for an attentive eye. Inner part of the chest, lay a magnificent necklace that seemed to whisper secrets of a promise of shared memories million years. Its intricate design reflected an artistry long forgotten, with a locket that held an air of mystery.

The moment Ebube laid eyes on it, a glimmer of excitement sparked in her soul. She turned to Samanpa, her eyes filled with anticipation, Samanpa urging her to try the necklace on. "It belongs to you," Samanpa insisted, her voice a mix of awe and urgency. With trembling hands, Ebube reached for the necklace, feeling the cool metal against her skin as she fastened it around her neck. In that magical moment, she felt connected to the echoes of the past, as if the weight of history rested lightly upon her shoulders.

The locket, once closed, now seemed to cajole with the promise of untold stories waiting to be unveiled. Ebube took the shining necklace and carefully clasped it around her neck, a radiant smile spreading across her face as the jewels caught the light. Samanpa, always the supportive friend, gently helped her adjust it to ensure it lay perfectly against her skin. The necklace, with its intricate design and vibrant colors, complemented Ebube's attire beautifully, enhancing her natural elegance. As she admired her reflection, the joy in her eyes was unmistakable. They both knew that this moment was special. It was not just a necklace; it was a symbol of friendship and shared experiences, marking another milestone in their journey together.

"You look absolutely perfect and magnificent in it."

"Thank you, Grandma Samanpa, for your incredible kindness. It means so much to me that you would allow me to try on something as precious as this. The experience is truly special, and I appreciate your generosity in sharing it with me. There's a certain magic in being able to wear something that holds such value and significance, and I feel fortunate to have this opportunity. Thank you once again for your graciousness; it has made this moment unforgettable."

"Don't be silly, my child," comes the soothing voice of wisdom, "you are far more precious than any glittering object your eyes may linger on or any dream your mind might conjure. Take a moment to reflect on your significance in the grand tapestry of existence, cherish your uniqueness and inner beauty, for you are a brilliant thread that enhances the whole. Always remember, you are a remarkable being, cherished beyond measure."

Ebube was still a child, her mind still absorbing the world in simple terms and bright colors. The complexities of adult conversations often flew over her head like birds on a clear day. However, one phrase that lingered in her thoughts was the proverbial utterance of Samanpa, a saying rich with wisdom and meaning, although, its depth was lost on her, she could still grasp fragments of the words that danced around her.

Ebube found solace in the innocence of play, unaware that one day she might unlock the secrets housed within those wise words, gaining insights that come only with experience and age. For now, the utterance of Samanpa remained an enigma, a clue to the mysteries she had yet to uncover in life. Ebube stood there, her heart racing as she marveled at the delicate necklace resting against her chest. It sparkled under the soft light, each gem reflecting a spectrum of colors that danced around her. Although she felt a wave of gratitude towards the woman who had permitted her to try on such a precious piece of jewelry, words seemed to escape her.

The weight of the necklace was not just physical; it carried a significance that made her acutely aware of its beauty and value. She felt both honored and unworthy, her mind racing with thoughts of admiration as she gently traced the intricate designs with her fingers. For a brief moment, time seemed to stand still as she immersed herself in this unexpected experience, lost in the dreamlike quality of the moment.

The necklace, a masterpiece forged by skilled hands, crafted from the finest materials, its complex design reflected artistry that transcended the ordinary. Each gemstone, carefully selected and expertly set, glimmered in a dance of colors, casting a spell of enchantment across the room, the townsfolk, though wealthy in their own rights, had never encountered anything quite like it; none owned a jewel that could rival its beauty. This necklace was not just an ornament; it was a symbol of exquisite beauty and an unattainable dream for many, a reminder of artistry that could only be imagined but never replicated.

CHAPTER FOUR

Many Suffer Long Who Are Not Long-suffering

As the moon dipped, casting a warm golden glow below the horizon, the air became thick with anticipation as she revealed more from a small, elaborately carved wooden box. The box's surface adorned with delicate patterns that seemed to dance in the fading light. With each passing moment, Ebube's eyes widened in wonder, eager to uncover more secrets nestled within. Just as the evening shadows lengthened, the bond between them grew stronger, kindled by the shared adventure that awaited inside the mysterious box.

Samanpa reached deeper into the chest, her fingers brushing against the soft fabric that protected the treasures inside. Amid the various trinkets, she pulled out a large, colorful book, its vibrant cover instantly capturing Ebube's attention. "Sit here and take a look at this," Samanpa urged, excitement radiating from her as she opened the fat book. Ebube's eyes widened in amazement at the book's sheer size. She couldn't help but wonder what stories lay within its pages. Ebube found herself mesmerized, eager to discover the secrets hidden inside this extraordinary tome. What kind of world would unfold before her?

The book seemed to hold secrets of its own, drawing both Samanpa and Ebube closer to its allure. Samanpa carefully opened the big colorful book, its pages filled with vibrant illustrations and intriguing text. She motioned for Ebube to sit beside her, eager to share the joy of discovery.

As Ebube settled in, she couldn't help but be mesmerized by the brilliant hues of the book. Her eyes widened with curiosity as she wondered about the wonders contained within its hefty spine. "Was it a storybook filled with adventures, or perhaps a treasure trove of knowledge?" She whispered. Each turn of the page promised new revelations, and the two were about to embark on an enchanting journey that would spark their imaginations and deepen their friendship.

Ebube gazed curiously at the enormous book Samanpa rested within the exquisite chest, its cover embellished with intricate patterns that hinted at the secrets held inside. "Grandma Samanpa;" she asked with a sense of wonder, "what kind of book is this?" The book seemed to emit an aura of mystery, its pages thick and worn, as if it had traveled through time and witnessed countless stories.

The beautiful chest, crafted from rich mahogany and lined with velvet, enhanced the allure of the tome it contained. Ebube couldn't help but be intrigued by the endless possibilities the book presented, ancient lore, or perhaps the wisdom of forgotten civilizations. Her imagination raced, and she felt an irresistible urge to uncover the treasures hidden within those pages, longing to embark on an adventure unlike any other.

Samanpa responded "The book is a profound tome that serves as a beacon of enlightenment for those who seek guidance in their lives. Its pages are imbued with timeless wisdom, offering insights that illuminate the often murky paths we navigate. Readers will find themselves captivated by its teachings, which encourage self-reflection and personal growth. As one delves deeper into its contents, the book unfolds layers of understanding, helping individuals to better comprehend their own journeys through its many lessons." Samanpa inspired a sense of clarity and purpose, making it an invaluable resource for anyone looking to enhance their outlook on life and find their way through the complexities of existence. In essence, she continued "this book is not merely for reading but for living, as it urges each reader to apply its wisdom and truth that will shine in their own unique paths."

Ebube asked "Just as the moon in all its majesty, was shining not just on my path but on my soul, illuminating the journey ahead with hope and wonder on my way here? "

"Yes, something similar to that," she replied, her eyes sparkling with excitement. "Tomorrow, I will read the story from this book to you by the bonfire." The promise of a cozy evening filled with stories made her heart race. She imagined the smoldering flames dancing in the cool night air, the enchanting tales woven within the pages of the book, and the thought of sharing them amidst the crackling fire filled her with joy. Tomorrow would be a perfect blend of warmth, friendship, and imagination, a moment to cherish under the starlit sky.

"Tomorrow, my dear child, I will share something truly special with you - a book that has the potential to change our lives. As we fish around into its pages, we will explore ideas that inspire and challenge us, igniting our imaginations and broadening our perspectives. Each chapter will open doors to new worlds and offer lessons that resonate deeply within our hearts. I promise to make this an enchanting experience, filled with laughter and thoughtful discussions."

"Why cant you read it to me today?"

"It is getting late and your folks might be worried sick not knowing where you were."

"I told them I was coming to thank you for saving me this morning so they know where I am."

"But they still will be wondering why you have stayed so long," Samanpa reassured softly, sensing Ebube's concern. "Don't worry my child; tomorrow, I promise to read you this life-changing book."

"Life changing book? can I please bring some of my friends with me to listen to this life changing book?"

"Of course, you can bring as many friends as you wish. Together, we will embark on a journey of discovery, transforming the way we see the world around us. So, rest easy tonight, knowing that our adventure awaits, and I can't wait to read with you. Just hold on to that excitement, for tomorrow will be a day of wonder and growth."

"Thank you, Grandma Samanpa; you truly are a wonderful person. Every moment spent with you feels like a treasure, and I often wish I could stay here by your side indefinitely. The connection we share is unlike anything I've experienced before, and it feels as though I have known you forever. Your kindness and warmth resonate deeply within me, and I find solace in our conversations. Each day with you brings new joy and laughter, and I am grateful for the memories we create together. In times of uncertainty, your presence is reassuring, making even the simplest moments feel profound. I cherish this bond we have formed and look forward to the many adventures that lie ahead."

"In moments of doubt and uncertainty, take solace in the steadfast presence that surrounds you. You are never alone; I am always with you, guiding you through the tangles of life. Let go of your worries and fears, for they are but fleeting shadows in the grand shade of your existence. Always remember that you are more than what meets the eye, a being of infinite potential and boundless imagination. Your journey is not limited to what you see or what you think; it stretches beyond, into realms of possibility that you have yet to discover. Embrace your true essence and believe in the strength that lies within you, for you are destined for greatness. Trust in this truth, and let it illuminate your path."

As the moon illuminated the night sky with an unprecedented brightness and size, it cast a magical glow over the fields. The duet, filled with joy, meandered through the tall corn-stalks, their laughter echoing in the stillness of the evening. With each step, they felt a sense of freedom, cool breeze gently brushing against their cheeks. The world around them seemed to sparkle under the moon's enchanting light, making every moment feel special. Their giggles intertwined with the soft rustle of the corn, creating a melody that celebrated the simple pleasures of life. In that luminous embrace, they were not just walking through a field; they were sharing a memory that would linger in their hearts forever.

Samanpa walked back home, her heart bursting with joy. The smile she had managed to bring to Ebube's face was a moment she had longed for, a dream she had nurtured for what felt like ages. As she strolled through the familiar path, the warmth of her achievement overwhelmed her, lightening up the evening sky.

Memories of past attempts kindled in her mind, reminding her of the challenges she had faced. But today was different; today, her efforts had finally paid off. The thought of seeing Ebube's happiness filled her with an indescribable sense of fulfillment and hope. With each step, she relished the sweetness of the moment, knowing that sometimes, the simplest gestures could create the most profound impact. Samanpa's heart danced as she envisioned the bond they would continue to build, filled with laughter, understanding and unbreakable joy. In a flurry of excitement, she raced into the little magnificent room, her heart pounding with anticipation. With trembling hands, she opened the ornate chest and unearthed the ancient necklace. As she stepped outside, the silver light of the bright moon seemed to beckon her closer, carefully, she opened the locket, revealing its intricate design, and tilted it toward the sky, as if offering its secrets to someone beyond the stars.

Momentarily, something extraordinary happened - the moon, the stars, and the sun aligned in a breathtaking display, a cosmic spectacle that felt like a celestial acknowledgment of her gesture. It was as if the universe itself recognized the significance of this connection, binding her destiny to the ancient tale whispered by the necklace and the luminous sky above.

Ebube lay awake throughout the night, her mind swirling with thoughts of Samanpa. The day's events replayed in her mind like a vivid dream, each moment reminding her of the bravery and quick thinking that had saved her life that morning. How could someone so kind and selfless exist in such a chaotic world? Ebube felt a profound sense of gratitude, mixed with awe at Samanpa's steadfast courage. She had rushed into danger without a second thought, putting herself at risk to pull her from harm's way.

As the stars twinkled overhead, Ebube's heart swelled with appreciation for the bond they shared. In the quiet of the night she intended to express her gratitude and keep Samanpa's spirit of bravery alive in her own life. This newfound friendship felt like a lifeline, inspiring her to cherish every moment and face the challenges ahead with renewed strength. She couldn't shake the thoughts of the secret room hidden within her tiny house. No one, not even her closest friends, could have imagined that such a place existed. It was filled with ancient artifacts that whispered stories of the past, capturing her young imagination. But what fascinated her most was the stunning, exotic necklace that awaited her in that mysterious space.

As she slipped it around her neck, she felt a rush of wonder and delight; it was unlike anything she had ever seen in her short twelve years of existence. The necklace sparkled under the soft light, intertwining with her dreams of adventure and discovery. Each time she pondered that hidden treasure, her heart raced with excitement, longing for more secrets to unveil within the little house she called home. Slowly, the weight of her eyelids grew heavier, and the gentle tug of sleep beckoned her.

Just as the final fiery of her imagination began to fade, she surrendered to the embrace of a slumber, leaving behind a world filled with wonder and dreams yet to be realized. In that quiet moment, she found peace, ready to explore new realms as she drifted into the unknown.

The early morning sun filtered through the trees as Ebube made her way to school, her heart still fluttering from the unforgettable encounter with Samanpa. Eager to share her extraordinary experience, she gathered her friends during recess and animatedly recounted the details of her visit.

"You won't believe how rich she is!" Ebube

exclaimed, her eyes wide with excitement. She described the lavish decorations and the exquisite artwork that adorned Samanpa's home, painting a vivid picture of opulence that left her friends in awe. As she spoke, her classmates leaned in closer, hanging on her every word, captivated by the life of Samanpa. Ebube excitedly shared the news with her friends about the Storybook that had been promised to her. She recalled how she had eagerly anticipated the moment when she would gather her closest companions for a delightful reading session. The thought of sitting together, immersed in the enchanting tales of the Book, filled her with joy.

She envisioned the warm atmosphere, filled with laughter and curiosity, as they listened attentively to each word. Ebube couldn't wait to create beautiful memories with her friends, all while exploring the magical world contained within the pages. The promise of adventure and good fellowship made the experience all the more special, and she felt grateful for the opportunity to include her friends in this wonderful journey.

The children buzzed with excitement at the prospect of the fat Book by a woman who seemed to exist in a world entirely different from theirs. Eagerly awaiting nightfall when they could gather around to hear Samanpa read. Though they had listened to storybooks before, this time felt special; their curiosity was piqued by the recent events.

Samanpa, a mysterious lady who had miraculously healed Ebube with nothing but juice from some leaves, held a magical allure. They imagined the tales she would intertwine, filled with adventures and characters that would take them far beyond their simple countryside.

As dusk approached, their anticipation grew, the spark of hope lighting up their faces. The thought of a story told by someone with such remarkable abilities made the evening feel like a wondrous adventure waiting to unfold. Adventure was just a story away, and they couldn't wait to delve into the mysteries of Samanpa's enchanting world.

That evening, the children were filled with excitement as they worked hard and fast to finish their chores. They knew that completing their tasks was essential to gain their parents' approval for a special adventure. Each chore was done with diligence and speed, as they eagerly anticipated the reward that awaited them. They longed to climb up the hill to gather around and listen to what was in Samanpa's Storybook, a treasure trove of tales that sparked their imaginations. With every sweep of the broom and every dish washed, they envisioned the stories that would transport them to distant lands and magical realms. Their teamwork and patience paid off, as they finished just in time, ready to embark on their journey up the hill and into the enchanting world of Samanpa's stories.

Back at Samanpa's house, the air was crisp with the promise of an enchanting evening. She busied herself gathering firewood for the bonfire, each log echoing the warmth she hoped to share. As she stacked the wood meticulously, an anticipation bubbled within her, as if she were preparing not just for a fire, but for the rekindling of stories that had long lingered in the shadows. It felt to her like this story reading was long overdue, a much-needed reprieve from the humdrum of daily life. The burning flames would soon dance to the rhythm of ancient tales, drawing friends and families together, weaving connections through the magic of words. Samanpa smiled at the thought, her heart swelling with joy at the idea of sharing cherished moments around the fire, where every story would spark laughter and create memories to last a lifetime.

As the sun dunked below the field of view, she arranged chairs in a cozy circle around the glowing bonfire, ensuring that every child had a front-row seat for the evening's storytelling adventure. With thorough attention, she prepared the drink, ensuring each ingredient was measured just right.

As she poured the concoction into the special clay pot, she whispered a small affirmation to herself, believing that this unique vessel would do more than just maintain the drink's coolness. The clay, with its earthy essence, promised to enrich the beverage, infusing it with flavors that would dance on her palate. Most importantly, she felt the pot held the potential for healing, transforming her simple drink into a remedy for both body and spirit. It was a sacred ritual, one that connected her to tradition while nurturing her well-being, as she anticipated the refreshing experience that awaited her. While she covered the drink, a sense of anticipation filled the air. The cups, each uniquely designed for the children, sparkled with a playful charm, She cautiously washed each one, imagining the delighted faces that would soon gather around her, ready to embark on an adventure through the pages of the Book.

The thought of sharing stories made her heart race; she wished she could fast forward time, skip past the mundane moments, and dive straight into the magic of reading. In her mind, the characters were already coming to life, and the children would soon be lost in worlds of imagination, united by the simple pleasure of a story. The clock seemed to tick slower, heightening her eagerness for the laughter and excitement that awaited.

Samanpa had a remarkable ability to gauge the time of day. This ability rooted not in any mystical powers but in her deep understanding of the relationship between the sun and the shadows it cast. She observed how the sun's position in the sky influenced the length and direction of the shadows, allowing her to estimate the hours without needing a clock. Whether it was the stretch of the morning light or the elongated shadows of dusk, she could sense the passage of time through these natural signs. This connection to the rhythm of the day gave her a unique perspective, filling her with a sense of harmony and awareness of the world around her. In a way, Samanpa lived in sync with nature's calendar, finding beauty in the simplicity of shadows dancing under the sun's watchful gaze.

Samanpa barely had time to close and open her eyes before the children began streaming into her house. With a warm smile, she ushered them into their seats, her heart swelling with joy at their excitement. As they settled in, she couldn't help but share in their enthusiasm. Samanpa took her own seat, rubbing her hands together in anticipation. Closing her hands tightly, she blew gently into them, a playful gesture that sparked laughter among the kids.

The air beneath the tree was electric with

energy, a blend of laughter and chatter as they prepared for the fun activities ahead. It was a delightful scene, one that filled her with happiness and reminded her of the simple joys of bringing children together for a day of laughter and learning. Excitement buzzed in the air as she announced her plan - not only would she read from her cherished Storybook, but she would also surprise her young audience with her favorite drinks, each infused with special ingredients that she kept as her own little secret.

The flaring flames cast playful shadows as she began weaving her tale, while the children sipped their enchanting beverages, their eyes wide with wonder and anticipation. It was a magical night, where stories came alive and friendships blossomed under the starlit sky, all thanks to her thoughtful preparations and passion for sharing moments of joy. Samanpa felt an overwhelming sense of excitement as she prepared to read to the children, her enthusiasm radiating in every corner beneath the moon. Among them, Ebube captured her attention the most, her wide eyes sparkling with curiosity.

While the children settled down, each turn of the page was met with a mix of giggles and gasps, but it was clear that Samanpa's energy and passion for storytelling surpassed even the children's excitement. As she animatedly brought the characters to life, she couldn't help but feel a special bond forming with Ebube, who seemed just as captivated by the tales as she was in telling them.

CHAPTER FIVE

Chip Off The Old Block

"He who lies with dogs rises up with fleas." As she opened the book, the last child settled into their seat, the room buzzing with anticipation. Samanpa glanced around, observing the shimmer of moonlight reflected in each child's eyes, their gazes brimming with expectation and excitement. The atmosphere was electric, filled with the promise of stories yet to be told. Before speaking the first word from the pages, she took a moment to absorb the energy in the air and connected with each eager face before her. With a deep breath, she chanted the words of an ancient incantation, drawing them into the world of imagination and wonder. At that moment, time seemed to pause, allowing their collective dreams to intertwine, all waiting to escape into the vibrant tales that lay within the Book's embrace.

"Billions of years ago, in a time long forgotten", the atmosphere was filled with the soft echoes of children's heartbeats, so quiet that one could hear each rhythmic thump. "Among these innocent souls, there lived a strikingly beautiful Queen who reigned with kindness and grace. Her radiance was matched only by that of her stunning daughter, the rightful Heiress to the throne. Together, they inhabited a realm where peace and beauty flourished, captivating the hearts of all who beheld them. Their days were filled with laughter and dreams, as the Queen nurtured her daughter, preparing her for the responsibilities that awaited. In this idyllic kingdom, love and hope intertwined, setting the stage for tales of adventure and bravery that would outlast the sands of time.

The Queen stood as a paragon of strength and grace, the most powerful and beautiful Queen to ever grace the earth. Her radiance captivated all who beheld her, while her extraordinary powers eclipsed those of any other ruler. She commanded respect and admiration with a mere gaze, her beauty a mesmerizing tapestry woven from the very essence of allure. No realm could contest her dominion, for she was the embodiment of ultimate authority as well as the personification of ethereal beauty. Her reign was marked not only by the might of her powers but also by the elegance she exuded, making her a timeless figure in the hearts and minds of those who dared to dream of her grandeur. She reigned supreme, a living legend whose legacy inspired awe and reverence.

Queen Nyansa of the kingdom of Alkebu-lan was a remarkable ruler, embodying both beauty and strength. Her wisdom attracted visitors from far and wide, each seeking her guidance. Whether it was a matter of the heart or concerns of the land, her advice was tailored to fit the needs of those who sought her counsel. Under her reign, Alkebu-lan flourished, becoming a beacon of prosperity and harmony. The people revered her not only for her regal presence but also for her ability to understand and solve their problems, making her a beloved figure in their lives.

Queen Nyansa's legacy as a wise and benevolent leader continued to inspire, reminding everyone that true power stems from compassion and understanding. Queen Nyansa had an only child, a fact that had always intrigued the children in her kingdom." As Samanpa began to share tales of the Queen's reign, curiosity bubbled in the air. Just before she could reveal the next part of the story, a young girl eagerly raised her hand, her eyes shining with anticipation.

"Grandma, grandma Samanpa, please tell us, what was the name of the only child?" The room filled with whispers as the other children leaned in closer, their imaginations running wild with possibilities, Samanpa smiled gently, knowing that the answer held secrets of love, legacy, and the bond between a mother and her cherished

Heiress. All eagerly awaited her response, eager to unveil the stories that shaped the beloved Kingdom. Samanpa paused, a smile playing on her lips as she gazed at the curious faces of the children surrounding her.

"Children," she began gently, "do you know that when drumming is coming to your home, you don't run to meet it?" The children responded with a chorus of excitement, cries of "Eh, Grandma Samanpa! what does that even mean?" Her eyes sparkled with wisdom as she replied, "It means patience is a virtue."

A moment of understanding passed over the children, and they collectively murmured, "Ohhh," their curiosity aroused. With their minds open to learning, Samanpa continued her story, weaving tales of life's lessons, tradition, and the beauty of waiting for the right moment, each word punctuated by their eager nods and sparkling eyes, eager to absorb the wisdom from Samanpa.

"Nyankonton, Samanpa continued, the daughter of the magnificent Queen, was a splendid reflection of her mother, sharing both her beauty and grace. From the moment she came into the world, the Queen's heart swelled with pride for her child, feeling that the Princess embodied everything she herself had aspired to be.

Unlike many children, Nyankonton wanted for nothing; her life was filled with comfort and love, as she had every material possession and emotional support she could ever dream of. The Queen, known for her power and allure, found joy not in her own achievements, but in the promise and potential of her daughter.

This deep love led her to cherish Nyankonton more than she cherished her own status, a testament to the profound bond between them." As the children pondered this, one couldn't help but wonder why the Queen valued her daughter's existence so fiercely. Samanpa patiently explained to the inquisitive children that the Queen's pride in Nyankonton stemmed from a deeper understanding of power and legacy. Nyankonton's darker complexion symbolized strength, with the Queen recognizing that it could bestow even greater influence upon her Heiress.

In a world where lineage plays such a crucial role, every child is a living extension of their parents, carrying forth their essence and ambitions. Samanpa conveyed that, through children, parents achieve a form of immortality, as their stories, dreams, and identities are passed down. Thus, the Queen's pride was not merely about appearance; it was a profound acknowledgment of the potential that lay within her lineage, where each child's existence promises a continuation of their heritage and the power it holds.

The Queen's heart brimmed with affection

as she lavished Nyankonton with love, attention, and exaltation, transforming the once lonely throne room into a vibrant space filled with joy and laughter. Their bond went beyond mere companionship; it became a powerful alliance that bolstered the Queen's spirit and reign. In the presence of Nyankonton, the shadows of doubt and uncertainty faded away, replaced by a firm sense of purpose and connection. The Queen's fondness for her grew with each passing day, promoting a mutual respect and admiration that would be remembered throughout the kingdom. Together, they faced the world, emboldened by the love that blossomed between them. In a glowing kingdom, the little Princess, Nyankonton, enjoyed a life filled with wonder, but it was the Guardian, entrusted by the Queen, who ensured her days were sheltered from danger.

The Queen, wise and caring, bestowed upon the Guardian special powers designed to protect her beloved daughter from any looming calamities. With a gentle heart and a watchful eye, the Guardian led Nyankonton through enchanted gardens and secret hideaways, all while keeping a vigilant lookout for any threats. Their bond grew stronger with each passing day, woven by trust and affection, allowing Nyankonton to flourish in her world of magic, knowing she was safe under the watchful protection of her dear Guardian. Together, they danced through challenges, laughter echoing in the air, as the kingdom thrived under the care of its loving protectors.

Nyankonton was a Princess of remarkable intelligence and insatiable curiosity. Her ability to learn swiftly set her apart, earning her the admiration of all around her. The Queen, captivated by her daughter's brilliance and charm, cherished her as the love of her life, guiding her with gentle wisdom. Despite her extraordinary qualities, Nyankonton remained unaware of the true depth of her power and beauty. With every lesson learned and each question pondered, she began to unlock the potential within herself, though the realization of her own worth still eluded her.

In a world filled with expectations and grandeur, Nyankonton's journey was just beginning, promising a future where she would ultimately embrace the gifts that lay hidden within her.

The kingdom of Alkebu-lan stood distinct amid a vibrant spectrum of realms. It was commonly held that the other Kingdoms radiating their unique hues of red, orange, yellow, green, blue, indigo and violeta grandeur that overshadowed Alkebu-lan's own.

The people of Alkebu-lan, with their warm brown and dark complexions, carried a deep sense of pride in their heritage, even as they faced the prevailing belief that they dwelled in the shadows of their more colorful neighbors. Despite this perception, the essence of Alkebu-lan was intertwined with resilience and a rich culture, fostering a spirit that cut across mere appearances. In a world captivated by color, the heart of Alkebu-lan pulsed with stories waiting to be told, challenging the notion that beauty solely lay in vibrancy.

One day, Nyankonton strolled through the vibrant gardens alongside Mathomba. As they walked, curiosity sparked within her, and she turned to Mathomba, asking, "What do you think I am? Am I more beautiful than the children of the other world?" The young Princess shared her doubt, recalling how her mother, the Queen, often praised her beauty, yet she pondered if it was merely because she was the Queen's only daughter.

Mathomba smiled gently, responding, "My Princess, it is true that the Queen adores you dearly, and her praise reflects the beauty that shines from within you." Nyankonton felt a warm blush rise to her cheeks, grateful for Mathomba's reassuring words.

"Thank you, Lady Mathomba," she replied, her heart lightened by the affection and wisdom of her trusted companion.

CHAPTER SIX

Selling Hens On A Rainy Day

Nyankonton had always felt a sense of dissatisfaction with her kingdom, Alkebu-lan, and one day she found herself lost in thought, puzzled by what made the neighboring kingdoms seemingly superior. After much contemplation, an idea struck her: perhaps it was their vibrant colors that set them apart. Intrigued, she considered the nearby Redion Kingdom, where the people boasted striking red complexions.

Driven by curiosity and a desire for understanding, Nyankonton persisted to embark on a quest to visit Redion and witness firsthand the reason behind their perceived greatness.

Her heart pounding with excitement, ready to explore the enchanting world of different colors and cultures, hoping to uncover the secret that would enlighten her on what truly makes a kingdom thrive. Mathomba soon understood that Nyankonton's inability to embrace her true self would hinder her from fully accessing her powers. This realization sparked a dangerous plan in her mind; she began to plot a takeover of the kingdom if the Queen were to fall. She believed that Nyankonton lacked a deep understanding of her identity and the incredible strength that came from her true color. Unbeknownst to them, the Queen, possessing her all-seeing wisdom, was quietly observing Nyankonton's struggles and Mathomba's scheming whispers. As a master of both light and shadow, the Queen knew that the unfolding events would shape their fates, intertwining their destinies in unexpected ways.

While Nyankonton grappled with her self-discovery, Mathomba's ambitions loomed, threatening the balance of power within the kingdom. Mathomba encouraged Nyankonton to embark on her quest, filling her with excitement and eagerness.

Under the cover of darkness, they packed their belongings, ensuring that no whispers of their departure reached the ears of the Queen. The two shared a sense of urgency and thrill as they prepared for the unknown adventure ahead. With their hearts racing and spirits high, they set off into the night, leaving behind the comfort of their familiar surroundings. Each step felt like a leap into a world of possibilities, and Nyankonton was ready to face any challenges that awaited her. Little did she know that this journey would not only test her courage but also deepen her understanding as she navigated the trials and wonders of her quest.

As Mathomba and Nyankonton journeyed far from the kingdom, they stumbled upon a tree where a group of children were playing. Nyankonton, eager to join in the fun, approached them excitedly. However, the children seemed disinterested and aloof, leaving Nyankonton feeling rejected. She couldn't shake the thought that her different color might be the reason for their lack of enthusiasm. Longing to fit in, she wished in her heart to be red like the other children. To her astonishment, as soon as the thought crossed her mind, her skin transformed into a vibrant shade of red.

With her new color, Nyankonton's heart soared at the prospect of being accepted, eager to share laughter and joy with her newfound friends under the warm sun. As Nyankonton observed the vibrant red hue enveloping her surroundings, a sense of confinement washed over her. It dawned on her that her vision was limited, spanning no further than twenty centimeters in any direction. In this diminished world, the laughter and joy of other children felt distant and unattainable, echoing her own frustrations. Perhaps, she pondered, this was a glimpse into the hearts of children who longed for seclusion, hoping to escape the burdensome noise of companionship.

One of the children explained that the red ones were uniquely crafted, designed to experience the world in such an intimate manner that they could only perceive what was immediately before them. This strange reality offered little pleasure, leaving Nyankonton to grapple with the bittersweet awareness of her isolated experience amidst a colorful environment that felt all too limiting. She sat beneath the tree, her heart heavy with sadness as the other children abandoned her. Their laughter echoed in her ears, sharp and unkind, as they made fun of her. She longed to be like them, wishing she had been born with a different color, one that would have earned their affection and acceptance.

Alone with Mathomba, she felt the weight of loneliness press down on her, wrapping her in a cloak of despair. That night, despite the tears that stained her cheeks, she found solace in the gentle lullaby her mother, the Queen, had taught her. As she sang, the melody became a bittersweet comfort, a reminder of love that rose above the cruelty around her. Though the night was long, she clung to the hope that one day, she would be embraced for who she truly was.

As the moon began to shrink in size, casting a gentle silver light over the countryside, Samanpa sensed that the evening was drawing to a close. She gathered the children around her, their eager faces illuminated by the fading glow, and gently urged them to head home. "Tomorrow will be another day, my little ones, and it will bring more stories to share." The children exchanged glances, disappointment glistening in their eyes.

"Ahhh, Grandma Samanpa, please! we want you to continue," they chorused, their voices tinged with hope.

Grandma Samanpa smiled warmly at their

enthusiasm, knowing that her storytelling would be a cherished adventure they could all look forward to. With the promise of more tales to come, the children reluctantly began their journey home, the anticipation of the next day dancing in their hearts like the twinkling stars above. Grandma Samanpa made a promise that thrilled the children - she would teach them the song Nyankonton was singing the very next day.

As Ebube and the other children expressed their gratitude with heartfelt "thank yous," they set off toward their homes, eagerly anticipating the lesson to come. Samanpa walked with them to the middle of the road, her heart bubbling with delight. She couldn't help but notice the spark of excitement in Ebube's eyes, which also filled her with joy. The enthusiasm shared between them created a bond that exceeded generations, reminding her of her own childhood moments filled with music and laughter. It was a simple but beautiful evening, with the promise of new melodies hanging in the air, a testament to the joy that comes from sharing stories and songs.

That night, Ebube was consumed with thoughts about Nyankonton's desire to be someone else. Deep down, she questioned whether she had ever wished to embody another person. The more she pondered, the more restless she became, tossing and turning in her bed until sleep finally claimed her.

With the dawn came a flurry of activity; Ebube hurried through her chores, but her mind remained tangled in questions about Nyankonton and the mysterious song that Grandma Samanpa had promised them. What could Nyankonton possibly do next? The anticipation hung in the air, fueling Ebube's curiosity throughout the day as she navigated her tasks, an undercurrent of excitement driving her thoughts back to the promise of music and the intriguing choices of her friend.

As night descended, the moon shone brightly above, casting a gentle glow over the gathering. Samanpa busily collected firewood and expertly arranged it to create a crackling bonfire, the heart of the evening's storey-telling. She set up the chairs in a welcoming circular formation, each seat beckoning the children to join in the fun. As the familiar aroma of her beloved concoction wafted through the air, her excitement grew; the children always adored her special treat.

One by one, they began to arrive, their laughter and chatter filling the night. With warm smiles, Samanpa ushered each child to their seat, eager to begin an evening of stories, new song promised, and shared memories under the watchful eye of the full moon.

Ebube and her friends took their seats, excited whispers filling the air. Ekumfi, Mansa, Ewe, Fantse, Asantse, Dagomba, Sissala, Ahanta, Abura, Amanfi, and Assurba eagerly rubbed their hands together, anticipating the next act of the legendary Nyankonton. The atmosphere buzzed with excitement and curiosity, each child's eyes sparkling with wonder as they awaited the unfolding of the tale. Samanpa, known for her enchanting stories and magical prowess, was about to draw them into a world of adventure, leaving behind the humdrum of daily life. With their hearts racing and imaginations sparked, they were ready for whatever surprises lay ahead, united in their eagerness to experience the next chapter of the unfolding narrative.

Before Grandma Samanpa could speak, Ekumfi reminded her of the promise to teach them the special song that Nyankonton had learned from the Queen. With eager anticipation, the children gathered around, their eyes sparkling with excitement.

"Alright, children," Samanpa said, holding up her hand to quiet them, "before we dive into the song, we must first do something important."

The seriousness of her tone captured their attention."We need to honor the traditional rituals that come before music. So first, we must connect with our ancestors through a small prayer." The children nodded, understanding the significance of the moment. They closed their eyes and joined hands, ready to embrace the wisdom of their heritage before embarking on the joyous journey of learning the Queen's song.

Ahead of diving into the enchanting world of stories, Samanpa gathered the children around, her voice softly resonating as she recited a melodic chant.

This ritual not only set the tone for the storytelling session, but also wove a magical thread connecting the children to the tale that awaited.

Each line of the song carried a rhythm that captured their attention, and together, they breathed life into the moment. As the final notes echoed in the air, Samanpa felt the anticipation building in the children's eyes, ready to be transported to fantastical realms. The song, a warm and unifying embrace, proclaimed her role as the storyteller, ushering the children into a realm of imagination and wonder where anything is possible for the journey ahead. Now the song proclaimed Samanpa:

'Believe in Yourself,' For all things believe in Yourself first

'You have all things you will never find anywhere

'Power, riches and all other good things lie in Yourself

'Nature is in You and you are in Nature.'

After the song, Samanpa captivated the children with a heartfelt recitation that resonated deeply within their young hearts.

Samanpa - Story' Story

Children - Story is a Myth and a Myth is a Story

Samanpa - Story can be true

Children - Myth can be true

Samanpa - What is story for

Children - Story teaches us lessons from the past

Samanpa - If you dont know your past

Children - You are bound to repeat mistakes

Samanpa - What is a Myth for

Children - Myth is a story about nature that connects us to her.

The cadence of her recitation set the stage for the story to come, igniting their imaginations and preparing their hearts. The children eagerly gathered around Samanpa, their eyes sparkling with anticipation as she began to teach them the Queen's song. One by one, they repeated each line after her, their voices rising in cheerful harmony.

"Thank you, Grandma Samanpa," said Dagomba, a bright smile lighting up his face. He understood the song's message, which encouraged them to embrace their individuality and love themselves. It was a lesson wrapped in melody, one that resonated deeply with each child.

As the final notes faded, Samanpa looked at them with a twinkle in her eye and declared, "now the story continues!" With that, the children leaned in, ready to embark on another adventure filled with laughter, learning, and the joy of being themselves. Nyankonton felt a heavy weight in her heart as she wondered why the other children rejected her despite her vibrant red color. As days turned into weeks, each passing moment marked another change in her colors, yet hope faded with every new hue. This was her sixth transition, a kaleidoscope of vibrant shades that expressed her friendship, but still, none of the children embraced her. Despite the mesmerizing hues that adorned her, each little one, regardless of their own colors, turned away, leaving her feeling isolated in a world that should have been filled with friendship and joy.

The struggle to connect weighed heavily on her heart, as she wandered through the colorful playground, longing for the warmth of companionship that seemed just out of reach. She wandered through a vibrant picturesque, her zest to change colors reflecting her ever-shifting moods. With each attempt to adopt a new hue, a wave of frustration washed over her, leaving her feeling more lost than before. The shades of her dreams slipped away like petals in the wind, teasing her with their beauty yet remaining just out of reach.

Days passed, and she wore a frown that seemed to cast a shadow over her spirit. Mathomba, noticing her sadness, offered a glimmer of hope. She spoke of a distant territory beyond the river, where perhaps the children would embrace her for who she truly was. The idea sparked a hint of inquisitiveness in her, and she eagerly asked Mathomba if they could visit this new land soon. With a reassuring smile, Mathomba promised to guide her there whenever she felt ready. Soon after, Nyankonton realized that a new beginning might be just across the water, waiting to welcome her with open arms.

Before the sun rose, Nyankonton and Mathomba eagerly prepared for their journey to the next territory. Nyankonton felt a ray of hope that the children there would be receptive and friendly. As they set off on their adventure, they discovered a vast field of flowers, blooming in an array of colors. She felt a sense of peace surrounded by the gentle sway of petals and the soft hum of nature. They walked through the vibrant fields of flowers, where towering trees provided shade and beauty.

Butterflies danced gracefully above them, flitting around their heads and shoulders. Nyankonton paused to admire the delicate lilies blooming in the valleys, their beauty captivating her. She playfully blew bubbles that floated gently from the flowers. With each step, the anticipation of new friendships and discoveries fueled her adventurous spirits, making the world around her even more enchanting.

As Nyankonton and Mathomba entered the next territory, she was immediately enchanted by the beauty that surrounded them. The entire town was bathed in shades of blue. Nyankonton marveled at the stunning hues and couldn't help but wish her own kingdom could reflect such splendor. Just then, two children appeared, their blue skin and hair seamlessly blending with the enchanting view.

Captivated by their striking appearance, Nyankonton felt a deep yearning to share in their vibrant existence. Without hesitation, she dashed towards the children, her heart filled with a desire to join them in their joyful pastime of gathering flowers. She felt a heavy weight in her heart as she approached the blue children, hopeful to join them in their gathering of flowers. However, their unanimous and piercing "no" shattered her spirit, leaving her feeling dejected and confused. Unable to comprehend what she had done to provoke such rejection, she sought answers, only to be met with rude indifference.

Distanced from the hurtful remarks, she wandered further into the field, where her sorrow transformed into a gentle melody. As she sang to the flowers, a magical transformation occurred - the blooms began to flourish more vibrantly than ever. Soon after, surrounded by the beauty of nature and the sweet resonance of her voice, she realized that, despite the children's cruelty, the flowers embraced her warmth and companionship, reminding her that love and acceptance could still be found amidst the pain. Nyankonton pondered deeply, dreaming of joy as she considered the whimsical idea of becoming a flower. She yearned to dance among the vibrant blooms, so she wished with all her heart and transformed into a delicate flower. However, her delight quickly turned to despair as she observed the surrounding blossoms fading and withering, their vitality linked to her new existence.

Heartbroken by the sight of their decline, she

realized she could not bear to be the cause of their sorrow. With a renewed sense of purpose, she made another wish, longing to protect the beauty of the garden. In an instant, she became a child with radiant blue skin again, embracing a blue identity once more while cherishing the flowers around her, determined to love and uplift them without sacrificing her own happiness. Nyankonton felt a wave of sadness wash over her once more, her heart heavy with discontent. Mathomba, undeviating and helpful Guardian, tried to console her, suggesting, "take it easy, Nyankonton, perhaps the next town will bring better fortune." She reminded her of the beauty that bloomed around her whenever she sang, her voice enchanting even the most delicate flowers. Yet, beneath her comforting words, Mathomba harbored a secret joy, recognizing that each time Nyankonton turned against herself, she diminished her own strength. As her unhappiness deepened, Mathomba couldn't help but feel a sense of triumph, knowing that the more she struggled with self-acceptance, the less vibrant her spirit would become. This bittersweet dynamic between the two revealed the complexities of friendship, where support sometimes masked an inner conflict that emerged from contrasting desires.

Queen Nyansa sat in anguish, unable to tear her eyes away from the unfolding drama of her daughter's adventures. Each episode left her heart heavy with worry, as she witnessed the challenges that seemed to crush the spirit of her beloved Princess.

King Mara of Alkebu-lan, ever the voice of reason, gently urged his Queen to trust in their daughter's resilience. "Be patient," he advised, "she will find her way." Despite her instinctive resistance, Queen Nyansa grappled with the truth of his words. "I hate to admit you're right," she confessed, "but her struggles are weighing me down." King Mara encouraged her to redirect her thoughts, to find solace in the present. Yet, the Queen could not shake the concern for her daughter, whose journey toward self-discovery seemed to be paving a path strewn with emotional turmoil.

The caring confidante Queen sat quietly, lost in her thoughts, as she gazed at the distant towers of the castle. She understood that the Princess was on a journey of self-discovery, a vital process that would lead her to become the strong and vibrant woman she had to be, still, lingering worry gnawed at her heart like a persistent shadow. How long would it take for the Princess to find her true essence amidst the thorns of doubt and fear that surrounded her?

Each passing day seemed to stretch on endlessly, filled with uncertainty and longing. She wished to ease the burden on her, to whisper words of encouragement and love. Still, she knew this was a path the Princess must tread alone, a necessary part of her evolution. All she could do was wait and hope that the day would soon come when the light of the Princess's spirit would shine brightly once again.

Nyankonton found solace in the memory of the flowers that had once seemed to delight in her presence. Perhaps Mathomba was right; possibly, luck awaited her in the next town. Determined, she remained steadfast not to dwell on her loneliness or abandon her quest.

"Under the cover of night", Ebube, and her friends sat quietly, captivated by the story being told. Some wept softly, understanding Nyankonton's feelings of isolation and yearning for acceptance. As the bonfire wavered and began to diminish, clouds gradually obscured the moon, signaling the passage of time. Samanpa sensed the night growing older and gently urged the children to head home.

"Children," she began, "tomorrow is another day..." But before she could finish, the excited voices of the children chimed in unison, "and another day will be a storytelling day." The warmth of their enthusiasm filled the air, and Samanpa couldn't help but smile.

"Thank you, Grandma Samanpa!" they chorused, their love evident in every word. Ebube, bubbling with affection, rushed forward to give her a big hug, quickly followed by the rest of the children, each taking turns to embrace her. A sense of contentment washed over them as they made their way home, the promise of another delightful day lingering in the air. Each child bid her goodnight, their hearts full and dreams ready to unfold.

"At the witching hour", Ebube lay in bed, her thoughts swirling like a tempest. She couldn't grasp what might be plaguing Nyankonton; the young girl's troubles seemed so profound. Was it a curse, or merely a stroke of bad luck that had befallen her? The concept of luck and misfortune danced in her mind, leaving her both curious and unsettled.

As the moon cast shadows across her room, she held on that the following day would bring answers. Perhaps Samanpa, with her wise demeanor and understanding of the world, held the key to unraveling Nyankonton's struggles. With this thought, she finally managed to close her eyes, hoping for clarity in the morning light.

CHAPTER SEVEN

A Bull In A China Shop

"Enough is as good as a feast" Ebube woke up feeling more distressed than she had before going to bed, haunted by a terrible dream about Nyankonton. As she lay tossing and turning, she couldn't shake the feeling that she was becoming too emotionally invested in Nyankonton's struggle. Despite not having much in common with her, there was an inexplicable connection that made her wish the best for her. In the depths of her restless night, an idea began to take shape in her mind; plan that could help Nyankonton discover and appreciate her true self. This spark of inspiration filled her with a renewed sense of purpose, fueling her keen interest to reach out and offer the support Nyankonton desperately needed.

The next morning, Ebube woke up with an eagerness that bubbled within her; she longed to see the sun break through the horizon. As the dawn approached, she hurried through her morning chores, anticipation electrifying the air.

In her dreams, while the world around her was enwrapped in slumber, she had woven a new narrative for Nyankonton, a figure she admired. With vivid imagination, she pictured herself embodying Nyankonton, taking on the weight of her struggles and challenges. In this moment of creative metamorphosis, she felt empowered, ready to illuminate the darkness surrounding Nyankonton's plight. Little did she know, her thoughts held the power to shift realities, igniting hope where despair lingered. The sun's rays, when they finally graced the earth, would be a symbol of new beginnings, lighting the way for both Ebube and Nyankonton to forge their destinies anew.

Realizing her shortcomings as a blue girl, Nyankonton felt a wave of doubt wash over her. In her moment of despair, she sought counsel from Mathomba, wondering if it was time to abandon her quest for self-improvement. Nonetheless, Mathomba's encouragement reignited her optimism, urging her to persist until her mission was fulfilled. With renewed resolute, the two continued their journey, only to find themselves unexpectedly standing before a sprawling dense forest. Little did they know, the forest was not merely a natural obstacle; it had been conjured by Ebube's vivid imagination, adding another layer of challenge to their adventure. As they stood at the edge, Nyankonton's heart raced, ready to face whatever awaited them within the mysterious woods.

The sun was shining brightly the next morning, casting its warm rays over everything. Ebube along with her young friends rushed about, eager to complete their daily chores. As Ebube made her way back from the riverside, she spotted one of her friends and called out to her, "wait, wait!" she hurried to catch up, with curiosity sparkling in her eyes. "How was your sleep?" she inquired. Her friend responded, "It was unusual, but okay." Intrigued, Ebube pressed on, "why do you think it was unusual?"

The morning air was filled with laughter and chatter as they walked together, sharing their thoughts and stories, the sunlight immersed them in a golden hue and making their friendship feel even more special. Ebube's thoughts swirled with hope as she envisioned a brighter future for Nyankonton.

In her imagination, Nyankonton embarked on a journey of self-discovery, traversing the deep, shadowy paths of the forest. Suddenly, she envisioned a mischievous gathering of dwarfs, their tiny figures bustling along the woodland trail. One dwarf, curious and wise, turned to another and posed a thought-provoking question: "Does Nyankonton truly understand who she is at her core? Is she aware of Mathomba's genuine essence?" The second dwarf nodded thoughtfully, pondering the complexities of identity and self-awareness. As they debated, their conversation echoed through the trees, debating a medleys of wisdom and insight that resonated with the forest's ancient magic.

Ebube felt a surge of anticipation, believing that Nyankonton was on the brink of uncovering a profound truth about her life and her place in the world around her. As Nyankonton walked deeper into the forest, she couldn't shake the uncanny stillness that besieged her. The usual symphony of birdsong had been replaced by a haunting silence, while the wind, despite its strong gusts, failed to stir a single leaf. It was as if time had paused, and the very essence of nature held its breath.

Confusion gnawed at her, prompting her

to ponder the unsettling quiet surrounding her. "What dark foreboding had silenced the forest's vibrant life?" She scanned her surroundings, searching for answers in the shadows of trees that loomed like sentinels, guarding secrets only they knew. As she ventured further, her mind raced with questions, each one echoing in the dead air, waiting for a response that might never come.

As Nyankonton and Mathomba approached the expansive river, they were met with an astonishing sight. The riverbank was teeming with animals of every size and shape, from the tiniest critters to the grandest four-legged creatures. However, a visible sense of despair hung in the air; the animals seemed consumed by a deep sadness, as if they were mourning the end of the world. Some wailed in grief, their cries ringing through the tranquil surroundings, while others rolled helplessly on the ground.

The dwarfs murmured amongst themselves, their voices barely audible over the din of sorrow.

Undeterred by the chaos around her, Nyankonton felt a strong urge to uncover the source of their distress, prompting her to push past Mathomba and move closer to the troubled gathering. With each step, her strength of will grew stronger, eager to unravel the mystery that had gripped these creatures in such profound sorrow. As she approached the gathering of dwarfs, a sense of urgency filled the air. Keen and perceptive, inquired, "what seems to be the problem?" No matter how hard she pressed for answers, Choka, the leader of the dwarfs hesitated, bound by a vow of secrecy that left him reluctant to disclose their troubles.

Nyankonton, adept at unearthing hidden truths, was determined to unravel the mystery on her own. To distract her, Mathomba feigned a mishap, but her gaze locked with that of a familiar dwarf, a silent acknowledgment of their past collaboration. Mathomba, specialized in tricks and had successfully navigated power swaps before; Nyankonton was just another assignment in her seasoned career, and likely not the last. The dwarfs, seasoned allies in such delicate missions, knew the stakes were high, and together, they prepared to tread carefully in pursuit of a solution. Nyankonton felt an overwhelming sense of dread as she approached the water bodies where the ocean, river, and streams converged. To her horror, she discovered that all the fish were dying, their once-vibrant scales dulled and lifeless in the murky waters.

The situation was even more dire for the cicadas, who were trapped above ground instead of returning to their natural underground habitat. The cane rats, known for their tendency to stay above the surface, in a bizarre twist, found themselves in an unusual synchrony with cicadas. As the cicadas emerged from their underground slumber, filling the air with their distinctive sound, the cane rats also chose to make their appearance above ground. This unusual disruption in their natural cycle sent ripples of concern through the environment, suggesting an imbalance that threatened not only these two species but the delicate ecosystem that depended on their harmonious exchange. Nyankonton knew she had to act swiftly to understand the cause of this calamity and restore balance before it was too late.

Every 17 years, cicadas emerge from the depths of the earth, venturing into the world to witness the changes that have unfolded over time, gathering stories to share with Mother Earth. In contrast, cane rats, who frequently surface from their underground homes, must retreat below during this momentous cicada return. It is said that these two creatures are bound by a natural law, forbidden to coexist in the same realm at the same time. This delicate arrangement, crafted by Mother Nature herself, faced an unprecedented challenge as the anticipated upheaval loomed, casting doubt on the possibility of a smooth exchange between the underground and above-ground dwellers.

As tensions rose, it became crucial to find a solution, or risk triggering disaster for both species and the harmony of their intertwined existence. Nyankonton felt a surge of urgency as she learned about the looming mystic disaster threatening her land. In her heart, she knew that only the Queen possessed the extraordinary power to avert this calamity and restore harmony to nature. The thought consumed her: the Queen alone could mend what was broken and reclaim what had been lost. Regardless, the daunting distance between them posed a formidable challenge. How could she summon the Queen's aid? Desperation gripped her as she imagined a world thrown into chaos, where order needed to be reinstated at once. With each passing moment, she paced restlessly from the shore to the forest and back, her mind racing without solutions, knowing that time was slipping away and the fate of their world hung in the balance.

Mathomba tirelessly urged her to stay focused on their mission, reminding her that concerns of nature were secondary. "Nature can fend for itself," she insisted, highlighting the distance of the Queen, who could provide help but was far away. Her advice was firm; pursuing their quest was paramount, and interruptions were not desired. In stark contrast, Nyankonton felt an undeniable moral responsibility, questioning how a world could thrive if nature remained in disarray. She passionately articulated her belief that Nature is the very essence of existence, and that humanity must nurture it in return for its gifts.

"We are all caretakers of each other," Nyankonton emphasized, urging Mathomba to recognize the interconnectedness of their world and the natural environment. Her perseverance illuminated a larger truth: to ensure a harmonious world, they must also honor and protect the fabric of nature that sustained them all. Nyankonton felt a surge of desperation as she pondered her options, feeling lost in a world where nature was in peril.

Suddenly, inspiration struck her like lightning. With an exuberant scream of joy, she jumped up and down, her heart bursting with excitement. This enthusiastic display stimulated the interest of the dwarfs nearby, though Mathomba grimaced at her exuberance, the other inhabitants of the shore, including the dwarfs and the fairies, were taken aback by her sudden outburst.

Choka questioned her excitement, pointing out the dire state of nature around them. Nevertheless, Nyankonton was quick to clarify; her joy was not about the crisis but rather the revelation she had just experienced - she had discovered who could come to their aid in this moment of urgency.

In a moment of desperation, the crowd surged forward, their eyes filled with hope. "Who can save our world?" A thunderous voice echoed, a collective yearning for a hero tangible in the air. The anticipation rose as Nyankonton stepped forward, proclaiming, "me, me, me!" The animals and dwarfs watched in rapt attention, eager for the promise of restoration.

With enthusiasm, she began to chant a sacred song, her voice sounding through the gathering. Notwithstanding, as the melody faded, nothing miraculous occurred. The hopeful gazes turned to confusion, and soon, mockery replaced their admiration. Nyankonton felt a surge of sadness wash over her as she stood before the very beings she wished to save, grappling with the weight of the world's expectations and her own faltering powers.

CHAPTER EIGHT

A Mouse That Has But One Hole Is Soon Catch'd

In a world teetering on the brink of ecological collapse, she stood helpless, grappling with the unsettling thought that perhaps the Queen had stripped her of the very powers necessary to save nature. The weight of despair pressed upon her as she considered the grim possibility that this was the Queen's design. But that can't be, she thought, feeling the urgency of the situation preying on her mind. Extinction loomed large if nature continued to deteriorate.

Around her, the desperate cries of her friends reverberated, each plea punctuating her inner turmoil. "I've tried everything," she confessed, frustration boiling within her. "But there's nothing left in me to give." Committed to uncover the truth, she felt a sparkle of hope ignite, knowing that some answers still lay hidden, waiting to be discovered before it was too late.

In a furious confrontation, Nyankonto approached Choka, whose seemingly carefree smile only fueled her anger. "While I may not be able to take your head, I can certainly silence those mocking lips," she declared, closing the distance to Choka with an intensity that was perceivable. Her words dripped with disdain as she challenged him, questioning his audacity to think she could not save nature.

"I was born to restore balance; I am a vessel of Nature's Will, The Princess destined to mend what is broken," she proclaimed, her confidence unchanging. Conversely, beneath her fierce exterior lay a shimmer of doubt, hinting that perhaps even the strongest convictions could be challenged.

"You think you can deceive me? Psss,

you could have fooled anyone but me," he scoffed, the weight of his words resounding the battle between ambivalence and purpose in their fractured world. Choka strode out with a regal air, leading the troupe of dwarfs behind him in a solemn procession.

"I know the Queen and her most beloved Princess very well," he declared confidently. "You are a mere imposter!" Nyankonton responded defiantly, "how can you assert that I am not the true Princess? I am the one and only Heiress to the throne of the Land of Alkebu-lan, the daughter of Queen Nyansa and King Mara Budukuma. Your claim is utterly baseless!" After a moment of silence, she turned to the dwarfs, seeking answers for Choka's audacity. Be that as it, their fearful silence spoke volumes, leaving her more confused than ever. It was clear that beneath their fear lay secrets, shrouded in the very shadows they cast as they followed Choka, uncertain of the confrontation unfolding before them.

An intriguing challenge emerged: a request for a vivid description of royalty. "Alright, alright," Choka declared, leaning into the tensed atmosphere. "If you can honestly depict how Her Majesty the Queen and His Royal Highness the king appear, I will gladly reveal the reasons behind my earlier statements." Desperation and anticipation filled the air as the dwarfs exchanged knowing glances, eager to see if their lost Princess could rise to the occasion.

With a confident grin, Nyankonton stood before the gathering, radiating an air of assurance. "No problem," she declared, her voice steady as she prepared to delve into the description of the regal figures presented before her.

Nyankonton's eyes sparkled with enthusiasm as she began to describe the noble beings she called family. "In a kingdom where beauty and wisdom reign, the Queen stands as a paragon of grace and power. My dear mother, with her dark complexion and enchanting brown eyes, captivates everyone who has the privilege to behold her. Her gorgeously billowing hair complements her majestic presence, making her the most honorable monarch the world has ever known. She embodies kindness, graciousness, and mercy, nurturing all her children with a gentle heart. On the other hand, my father, the King, matches her allure with his own extraordinary features. Tall and robust, he possesses the same dark complexion and lovely brown eyes, making them an awe-inspiring royal couple. Their beauty and wisdom together create a family legacy that is both powerful and remarkable."

As she spoke, the crowd leaned in closer, captivated by the vivid imagery and the passion that flowed from her. Tension crackled between her and Choka, their uneasy exchanges thick with unspoken resentment. Each word felt like a weight, plunging the atmosphere into a noticeable gloom that plagued everyone present, leaving Choka, in disbelief at the rarity of such description. Is it really possible for two individuals to embody different features? Choka's voice trembled with disbelief as he repeated the word "impossible" "How can it be possible for the Queen and the King to produce an entirely different species?" He demanded, frustration boiling within him.

Like a mantra, Nyankonton's mind raced to grasp the absurdity of the accusation. "This has to stop!" she shouted, her eyes blazing with indignation. "You cannot speak of my parents in such a way. It is unthinkable." Nyankonton stood firm, determined to defend her identity against any unfounded claims that could tarnish her lineage. At that instant, surrounded by accusations, she longed for clarity, searching for evidence of her true heritage in a world that seemed bent on denying it. In her heart, she grappled with the loss of her once magnificent abilities, feeling a deep pang of uncertainty.

"Did you lose only your powers, or something more crucial?" he pressed, his voice laced with concern. She paused, contemplating his words.

"What do you mean?" She retorted, choosing not to entertain his musings about her likeness to the Queen. Instead, she found solace in a more profound purpose. Ignoring the doubts swirling in her mind, she focused on the task at hand—restoring nature, a duty that felt essential to her identity as a Princess. With excitement igniting her spirit, she began to chant her song once more, each note a promise to reclaim the power that once thrived around her. Her purposefulness was unyielding, for she understood that her true essence lay not in powers alone, but in her unfaltering commitment to her realm.

CHAPTER NINE

Many A Little Makes A Mickle

As the sun descended below the horizon, casting long shadows across the field of vision, the situation remained static. The air was thick with anticipation and uncertainty, while the forest around them held its breath. Mathomba approached her, emphasizing that it was time for them to press on with their vital quest . Nyankonton reminded Mathomba of the paramount importance of saving and restoring nature. "What could be more important than saving and restoring nature? If we fail in this mission, there would be no adventures left to pursue." She felt overwhelmed and needed a moment to herself, so she parted ways with them and descended into the dark caves of the Dwarfs.

Choka reached out, grasping her arm firmly,

and said, "you can't walk away from this mess until it's fixed." His words lingered in the air, resonating the urgency of their task. The weight of the quest pressed on her shoulders, reminding her that every step forward meant a step closer to healing the world, and perhaps, to finding herself along the way.

As she wandered through the serene forest, the Princess of Alkebu-lan felt the weight of her quest bearing down upon her. The words of her people echoed in her mind, reminding her of the delicate balance between the water and ocean, a balance she was destined to protect. But amid her responsibilities, she grappled with her own identity, desperately trying to be something she was not. She had tried to embrace colors that didn't resonate with her soul; red, orange, yellow, green, blue, indigo, and violet, yet each choice had led her further away from her true self.

With a heavy heart, she sought the forgiveness of her beloved mother, the Queen, realizing that to reclaim her identity, she needed to accept who she was rather than chase after ideals. At that instant of clarity, the Princess understood that her strength lay not in transformation, but in embracing her authentic self. As she reminisced about her childhood, a vivid image of a heart-to-heart conversation with the Queen filled her mind.

She recalled the Queen's warm words of wisdom: "No matter what life throws at you, cherish your true self and embrace your individuality, for there is so much more within you than meets the eye." Overwhelmed with emotion, she broke down in tears, longing to reconnect with her authentic self. In an instant, Nyankonton felt the transformation, returning to her original form. With newfound clarity, she called out to the others, sobbing yet hopeful, urging the creatures in the forest and beyond to gather around her once more. This moment of unity and self-acceptance marked a turning point, a reminder of the strength that comes from being true to oneself amidst life's challenges. As the once-lifeless creatures in the water began to stir, they turned to the enigmatic figure before them.

"Who are you again?" they asked, their voices a whisper of hope.

"I am Nyankonton," she replied, her voice steady and resonant. "Once, I lost my way, but never again will I stray from myself. We must save nature and restore the law of order." With that, she began to chant her song, a melody so powerful that it reverberated through the depths of the earth and water.

Slowly, vitality returned to the fish, their colors brightening, while the animals around them found renewed energy. The cicadas rejoiced, ready to emerge once more after 17 long years, while dolphins leaped joyfully from the waves, celebrating their rebirth with playful hisses. Nature, once again, danced to the harmonious rhythm of life. In a joyous gathering, all the animals expressed their gratitude to Nyankonton for saving nature and restoring balance to their world. The trees swayed gently as birds filled the air with their melodic chirps and songs, celebrating the returned harmony.

Nyankonton turned to Choka, pondering why she had never been informed of her uniqueness. "If nature had perished completely, it would have been your fault," Choka quickly exclaimed dismissing the notion with an assertion, "I never sought to change; the responsibility lies solely on you!" The conversation lingered in the air, highlighting a deep sense of misunderstanding and the weight of accountability. Nyankonton, in search of answers, wondered about Mathomba's silence.

"Mathomba, where are you?" She called out, hoping for clarity in a moment filled with confusion and unspoken thoughts, reflecting the complexity of their intertwined fates in a world now on the mend.

Mathomba had completed her mission; Nyankonton had rediscovered herself, and her journey was just beginning. With an eye on the throne, Mathomba knew that the Queen had orchestrated a departure meant to distance her from the Princess. The silence surrounding this plan felt heavy, leaving many to wonder why no one spoke up. Yet, it was a time for discovery and revelation, and fortunately, Nyankonton arrived just in time to save nature from impending doom.

As Choka and Nyankonton embraced, they exchanged heartfelt goodbyes. "Our job here is done," Choka said. Pride shimmering in her eyes. "Nature has been restored." He encouraged Nyankonton, confident that she would rise to greatness, even if it meant stepping into the formidable legacy left by her mother.

"Good luck," Choka added, "but remember,

those shoes are quite large." With that, the future Queen took her first steps toward destiny.

Back at the palace, the atmosphere was jubilant as the Queen and the King reveled in their newfound happiness. The turn of events had brought joy and satisfaction that brightened every corner of their regal residence. As they strolled through the opulent halls, laughter echoed off the walls, a stark contrast to the tense days that had preceded this moment. Delighted whispers floated among the courtiers, and a sense of celebration filled the air, with preparations already underway for a grand feast. The royal couple exchanged glances, their eyes sparkling with optimism for the future. They had faced challenges together, but now, hand in hand, they looked forward to a brighter chapter in their reign. It was a time for unity and joy, where every heart in the palace seemed to beat in harmony with the happiness that surrounded them.

As Samanpa continued with the story, she

noticed Ebube's ecstatic reactions, which were hard for her to contain. It struck Ebube that the tale unfolding before her was precisely what she had envisioned the previous night. Samanpa, with her keen insight, had already discerned that the transformation of the book was influenced by none other than Ebube, whose unique gift could turn imagination into reality. A playful shrug from Samanpa conveyed her understanding, and their eyes met in a shared moment of joy. The two exchanged friendly smiles, with Samanpa feeling happy and relieved that Ebube had finally embraced her incredible potential. It was evident that this was a talent that could not be learned, but rather one that Ebube must unlock herself.

Encouraged by this newfound understanding, Samanpa eagerly continued with the tale, excited for what lay ahead. The children beamed with happiness, relieved that Nyankonton had finally discovered her true self just in time to save and restore nature.

Samanpa expressed that Nyankonton had come to understand the constant guidance of her parents about the importance of self-discovery. In an emotional farewell, she addressed the animals, creatures in the water, and the dwarfs, making a solemn promise to cherish them all.

With a heart full of gratitude, she shared that through a vivid spectrum of colors, she learned a profound truth: even in one's lowest state, it is far better to embrace who you are than to wish to be someone else. Her journey of self-acceptance resonated deeply, leaving a lasting impact on everyone present, who now understood that true happiness lies in recognizing and valuing one's unique essence.

In a world where individuality is often overshadowed by conformity, she created the vibrant "Nyankonton" (the rainbow), a breathtaking spectacle of colors she had transformed into. Each hue represented a facet of her essence, a reminder of the beauty in diversity.

As she painted the sky with her creation, she made a heartfelt promise - that whenever the Nyankonton (the rainbow) graced the heavens, it would serve as a beacon for all. No matter what challenges or states of mind they faced, the appearance of the Nyankonton (the rainbow) would be a gentle nudge to embrace their true selves. In doing so, she hoped to inspire everyone to cherish their uniqueness and resist the pressure to become someone they are not, fostering a sense of belonging in a world that often encourages sameness. Through her colorful promise, she invited others to find strength in their individuality and celebrate the beauty of being themselves.

The children erupted in delighted applause, their faces beaming with joy as they rushed to give Grandma Samanpa big, warm hugs. "Thank you for the wonderful story!" they exclaimed, their eyes sparkling with excitement as they reminisced about the amazing ending that had captivated their imaginations. Eagerly, they pressed her about when they could visit again, hungry for more tales to fill their hearts with wonder.

Samanpa, with a twinkle in her eye, assured them that plenty of enchanting stories awaited them just around the corner. The promise of future adventures and cherished moments together filled the area with anticipation, as the children basked in the warmth of her love and storytelling magic.

The chill in the air reminded her that night was falling. She gathered her thoughts, summoning the courage to call to them. With a gentle smile, she waved them off, ensuring they ventured home safely, their playful chatter trailing behind like whispers of childhood. Watching them disappear into the shadows, she felt a bittersweet twinge in her heart. The night, once vibrant with life, now seemed to quiet around her, leaving only the lingering warmth of their laughter and the soft glow of the fading moon.

As she made her way home, a shooting star streaked across the sky, seemingly heading toward her house. A gentle breeze caressed her face, and in that split second, she felt a profound connection, a sign that the Queen was pleased with the recent changes in Ebube's life. Though she longed to share her thoughts with Ebube, the late hour reminded her it wasn't the right time. Maybe some other time, she whispered softly to herself. She finally bid Ebube good night, feeling a sense of warmth and hope.

Samanpa walked her almost to her door, and with a tender kiss on her forehead, she provided a sense of comfort and reassurance. As she entered her home, the beauty of the night remained in her heart, leaving her with a sense of peace and optimism for the future.

CHAPTER TEN

All Is Well That Ends Well

"Better be bird of the wood than bird of the cage" As the days advanced into a quiet monotony, Samanpa found herself increasingly worried about Ebube, who had inexplicably vanished from her sight. It was on the fourth day, a serene Saturday morning, when a glimmer of hope reappeared.

Ebube rose early to visit the stream, committed to fill the water jars for her home before heading to Samanpa's house to do the same. By the time Samanpa awoke, she found her jars brimming with water and her home sparkling clean. "Oh my lovely child, thank you so very much for all you do for me," Samanpa exclaimed, showering Ebube with her customary words of kindness and blessings. In gratitude, she prepared a delicious breakfast for the two of them. As they settled down to eat, she looked at Ebube with concern and affection.

"How are you doing today, my darling child?" She asked, easing herself into her seat. "I have not seen you or heard from you in days now. That is very unusual of you." The warmth of their bond filled the cozy kitchen, ready to nourish not just their bodies but also their spirits.

Ebube replied to her with a hint of exhaustion in her voice, explaining the reason for her absence. "Yes, Grandma Samanpa," she began, "I've been quite busy these past few days." she elaborated that she had been occupied with packing up her parents' belongings as they were preparing for a trip to another town. The hustle of sorting through clothes, documents, and various household items consumed much of her time and energy. In fact, her parents had left early that very morning, just before she set off to the stream for a moment of respite. Ebube's dedication to helping her family shone through, even as she yearned for a brief escape into nature.

"Grandma Samanpa, do you recall the last time I visited? You were curious about my reasons for wandering through the cornfield."

"I can see the memory still lingers in your mind."

"Well, I must ask you to promise me something. Please, do not let anger cloud your heart with what I'm about to share. I know, I know, it's a big request."

"But how could I ever harbor anger against you, my dearest? I assure you that anything you reveal will stay locked between the two of us, just as cherished secrets should be. I'm ready to listen, and whatever it is, we will face it together, as we always have. You can trust that I will understand, no matter how difficult it may be."

"In our recent discussion about the Storybook, *Nyankonton*, I couldn't shake off the sadness I felt for her character. Despite her ability to transform into others, she struggled with self-acceptance and belief in her worth. That night, as I lay in bed unable to sleep, I imagined a different ending for her - a journey where she learns to appreciate herself and recognizes the power within her. To my astonishment, when I revisited the story, it mirrored the outcome I had envisioned. It felt surreal, as if my imagination had intertwined with the narrative, shifting Nyankonton's path towards self-discovery. I didn't expect such a connection between my thoughts and the storyline, but it opened my eyes to the magic of storytelling and the potential that lies within every character, waiting to be unveiled. Please forgive me if my imagination took liberties with the tale."

Ebube's heart swelled with gratitude as Samanpa reassured her, dismissing any need for apology. The warmth in Samanpa's voice gave Ebube the strength she needed, allowing her to relax and take a breath. Clutching the book against her side, she took a moment to regain her composure, still feeling the weight of their earlier conversation. Just as she was about to speak, an overwhelming surge of joy bubbled up inside her. In a spontaneous burst of affection, Ebube leaped forward, wrapping her arms around Samanpa in an exuberant hug. Their shared smile spoke volumes, a silent affirmation of their bond, leaving both of them feeling uplifted. In that brief yet profound moment, they knew they had each other's backs, united in their triumphs and struggles, nurturing a friendship built on understanding and love.

As Ebube rested her head on Samanpa's shoulder, a book slipped from her hands, and a photograph fluttered out, landing softly on the ground. Samanpa's eyes sparkled with a knowing glint as she did not shy away from the unexpected reveal. With a gentle turn, she faced Ebube directly and said, "this is yours." She handed the photo over, revealing its significance. Samanpa explained that it was part of a cherished chest meant for her at the right moment. "I'm giving these to you as they are," she continued, filled with sincerity, "with my best wishes for a happy self, an excellent reign, and utmost fulfillment."

The weight of the moment hung in the air, blending nostalgia with hope for the future, as Ebube realized the importance of the gift being presented to her, she jumped down to retrieve the photograph, her excitement quickly transformed into astonishment. "Oh, how kind, how kind," she exclaimed, her eyes scanning the contents with a mix of curiosity and remembrance. In the picture, a younger version of herself beamed joyfully, her innocent smile reflecting the untainted happiness of a child's carefree life. Beside her, her parent radiated a sense of pride and love, their arms wrapped protectively around her small frame.

The old photograph whispered stories of

laughter, moments spent playing in the sun, and the indestructible bond shared. evoking a bittersweet wave of sentiment as she reminisced about the 'would have, could have' moments of her life. This little child looks like me, she whispered, captivated by the image. Meanwhile, Samanpa, who had been quietly observing, refrained from revealing the truth about her long-ago assignment to aid Ebube in navigating her past. The moment was filled with a bittersweet connection to a time long forgotten, merging the innocence of childhood with the complexities of memory and identity.

Ebube was born into a royal family, heralded with great celebration, as she stood as the sole Heiress to a magnificent legacy. The day she was crowned as the sole Heiress marked not just a pivotal moment in her life but also the beginning of a new era for the kingdom. Even at an age when most children are preoccupied with toys and games, Ebube found herself seated upon the throne, bearing the weight of responsibility and expectation. Nobles from across the land gathered to pay their respects, kneeling before her in acknowledgment of her status and the promise of leadership she embodied. As she contemplated upon her court, young yet resolute, Ebube understood that her path had been set, and the grand tapestry of her royal destiny awaited her to weave it with wisdom and grace.

Ebube, the lonely Princess, often found solace within the confines of her kingdom, yet her heart yearned for companionship.

One fateful day, her Guardian, under the guise of friendship, led her astray with promises of a playmate. Struggling with the weight of her title and the isolation it brought, she longed for a connection that seemed perpetually out of reach. Her mother, the Queen, always attempted to soothe her distress, reminding her that she must embrace her feelings to truly discover herself. "You must not feel this way, my Princess," she would say, "for one drop of ink may make a million think." As the Queen's words echoed in her mind, Ebube grappled with her loneliness, unwittingly stepping into a dangerous game that would challenge her understanding of trust and vulnerability. Little did she know, the world outside her kingdom held both peril and unexpected friendships waiting to unfold.

Ebube eagerly anticipated the royal celebrations of her birthdays and Christmases, when the Queen would invite all the children of the kingdom to the palace. These joyous occasions provided a brief respite from her loneliness, filling the palace with laughter and warmth. The Queen reveled in the festivities, but even surrounded by laughter and cheer, her longing for a larger family remained unfulfilled.

The generous offerings from the royal household brought happiness to many, yet once the celebrations ended, Ebube felt the familiar weight of solitude creeping back into her heart.

Though the festivities were a highlight in her year, they served only as a temporary balm to her loneliness. As the sounds of laughter faded, Ebube found herself awaiting the next celebration, hoping that perhaps one day, she would find the connection she so deeply desired.

One day, a peculiar man wandered through the open gate of the palace and leaned against a nearby tree. His worn, dust-gray clothes contrasting starkly with the grandeur around him. His haggard face hinted at a troubled past. Suddenly, a strange noise drew her attention to the fence, where she caught sight of her captive - none other than her own Guardian. Heart aching, she whispered, "help, please save me from this old haggard."

Tears streaming down her cheeks. "don't cry," he replied gently, "my little girl would be just your size." Surprised, Ebube asked, "would she?" As she sat quietly, her mind drifted to thoughts of friendship with his child she longed to meet. A glimmer of hope sparked in her heart, brightening her otherwise weary spirit. She imagined the joy that would fill her days, the laughter that would ring through the halls, and the tender moments they would share. As she sat alone in her new surroundings, a wave of homesickness washed over her.

Clutching her beloved doll, tightly to her chest, she could almost hear the laughter of her parents in the yard. Though she tried to immerse herself in this new chapter, the ache for home never faded. "No one would know where I am," she murmured, the weight of her words heavy in the air. The thought of her mom and dad sent waves of remembrance crashing over her, and she repeated, "I want to go home to my mom and dad." A cold and dismissive response echoed: "It's too late. Mom and Dad can't help you. You will be home in a little while, but for now, you are all mine." Those final words echoed ominously, a stark reminder of her uncertain fate. Soon after,

Ebube realized that this might indeed be the last time she would ever voice her yearning to return to the warmth of her family's embrace.

Her journey took her far from home, away from the familiar faces she once cherished. Unaware, Samanpa had been sent on a mission long before, destined to meet her at this very moment. As a prepared missionary, Samanpa came to illuminate the dark corners of Ebube's heart, filling her life with hope and purpose. Though she carried the weight of being the throne's sole Heiress, the trials she faced were part of a grand design to help her discover her true destiny. In her solitude, she would learn to value her youthful impulses, nurturing the vibrant spirit within her. It was the Queen's wish that one day, her young Princess would radiate a brilliance so profound that all obstacles would dissipate, unveiling a sky as clear and joyous as the sunniest of days.

Ebube sat quietly, her mind swirling with

thoughts of her encounter with Grandma Samanpa. Her words echoed in her ears, especially the reminder of the unique power of solitude: "Lonely hands can go to places where many hands can't go." Those parting words weighed heavily on her, illuminating the depth of her mission and the solitude it entailed.

As she lay in bed that night, the stars twinkling through her window, Ebube pondered the significance of her journey. What did it truly mean to walk alone, yet so profoundly connected to a greater purpose? The Queen's explanation had unlocked something within her, a mix of fear and excitement. This pivotal moment stirred her spirit, and she realized that embracing her solitude could lead to extraordinary discoveries. With her heart pounding and thoughts racing, sleep eluded her, as visions of her mission danced in her mind.

As Samanpa sat by the window, the sunlight filtering through the leaves danced across her thoughtful face. She had been lost in deep reflection, considering the Queen's words about the significance of her mission. The weight of the responsibility rested heavily on her heart, but it also ignited a flicker of anticipation within her.

Ebube equally found herself unable to sleep, haunted by Samanpa's enigmatic farewell. "remember, lonely hands can go to places where many hands can't go," Samanpa had said, the words echoing endlessly in her mind. As she rummaged through old photographs and a forgotten necklace in a chest, a whirlwind of questions engulfed her. Who was she, really? How could she reconnect with her roots? Samanpa's cryptic messages left her feeling adrift, igniting a desire for understanding. The tale of Nyankonton, the lone seeker, played repeatedly in her thoughts. Perhaps, like Nyankonton, she was destined to embark on a solitary journey of discovery, unraveling the threads of her identity and heritage, one enigmatic clue at a time.

Upon settling down, Samanpa stood poised to sing another tune, the air around her filled with a calming pitch and soothing rhythm. Despite the joy in her voice, a quiet awareness lingered within her; she understood that her time on Earth was drawing to a close. Suddenly, two glowing orbs materialized, swirling gracefully around her. At that instant, she was united with her beloved, who had guided her through life with unbreakable love. Together, they were covered by the radiant spheres, taking her on a journey beyond the constraints of time. Immortality was calling, promising a harmonious existence free from the sorrows of the earthly realm. The melody of her life continued, echoing in the eternal embrace of love and light.

Ebube felt exhilarated yet anxious about the newfound truth regarding her identity. Questions swirled in her mind about her future and the path she would take. Despite the uncertainties, one thing was crystal clear: she would not allow herself to be despised, ridiculed, or discouraged by anyone. Instead, she resolved to approach this journey with diligence and hope, understanding the importance of self-discovery before time and failing sight could dim her aspirations.

With a firm belief that patience would eventually lead her to what she desired. Ebube was ready to embrace the challenges ahead, armed with hope and resilience. She knew that each step forward would bring her closer to understanding herself fully and living life on her own terms.

ACKNOWLEDGEMENT

To my cherished readers, I extend my heartfelt gratitude for welcoming me into your lives and permitting me to explore the depths of your thoughts. Your support and engagement inspire me to share my reflections and stories, creating a bond that transcends mere words on a page. Every comment, every shared experience enriches my writing journey, reminding me of the profound connection we share. Together, we navigate the complexities of life, finding common ground in our hopes, dreams, and challenges.

Thank you for your trust and for allowing me the privilege of using my words to resonate with your minds and hearts. It is an honor to be a part of your world, and I look forward to our continued adventure together through the written word.

ABOUT THE AUTHOR

Ama Nkrumah

Ama Nkrumah, a novice fiction author who writes captivating stories coupled with richly developed characters. With a background in philosophy, and a passion for storytelling, she intricately weaves human emotions into her narratives, making readers feel a profound connection to her characters.
Ama Nkrumah's ability to create immersive worlds, combined with a flair for suspense, keeps readers eagerly turning pages.

After years of nurturing her dreams, countless hours spent crafting characters and weaving intricate plots, the moment felt surreal. Her book, a reflection of her innermost thoughts and experiences, was finally out in the world, ready to be discovered by readers. This journey is just the beginning, a stepping stone towards her aspirations of becoming a celebrated author. With a heart full of hope and determination, she is eager to share more stories that would resonate with others and leave a lasting impact.

NYANKONTON BE YOURSELF

"If a man be not enlightened within, what lamp shall he light?" Nyankonton, despite her immense power and abundance, embarked on a perilous journey driven by a profound lack of self-awareness. She quickly learned that her quest was akin to jumping from the frying pan into the fire, facing challenges that tested her resolve. Through her trials, she discovered that time progresses relentlessly, much like an arrow shooting through the air. This realization was coupled with the understanding that, just as no ten fingers share the same length, every being has its unique purpose to fulfill. Nyankonton's journey became one of self-discovery, as she began to appreciate the distinct roles that each individual, including herself, plays in the grand tapestry of existence.

In a moment of reckless abandon, she tossed a stone into the well, the very source of her sustenance, unaware of the chaos it might unleash through the influence of her malicious Guardian. Time was of the essence, and the fate of the universe teetered on the brink of disaster. Yet, amid the uncertainty, a flicker of hope remained. As she grappled with the gravity of her choices, she began to realize that the true power lay not just in her actions, but in her recognition of self-worth and resilience. With every moment counting, she was determined to harness the inner potential she had yet to fully embrace, for it was the key to saving not only herself but the entire universe.

www.ingramcontent.com/pod-product-compliance
Lightning Source LLC
Chambersburg PA
CBHW071248130626
46556CB00003B/1221